High praise for bestselling author **LAWRENCE BLOCK**

Winner of every major international award for crime fiction, including America's Edgar® and Great Britain's Cartier Diamond Dagger

"Block is awfully good, with an ear for dialogue, an eye for lowlife types, and a gift for fast and effortless storytelling."
Los Angeles Times

"A first-rate writer."
Chicago Sun-Times

"Lawrence Block is a master of ingratiating, literate entertainment."
Washington Post Book World

"One of the best writers now working the beat."
Wall Street Journal

"A very experienced practitioner who knows exactly what he is doing."
New York Times Book Review

"One of the better storytellers around in any genre."
Milwaukee Journal Sentinel

"One of the surest, most distinctive voices in American fiction."
Martin Cruz Smith

ME TANNER, YOU JANE

YOU JANE
AN EVAN TANNER NOVEL

LAWRENCE BLOCK

HARPER

An Imprint of HarperCollinsPublishers

This book is a work of fiction. Names, characters, places, and incidents are products of the author's imagination or are used fictitiously and are not to be construed as real. Any resemblance to actual events, locales, organizations, or persons, living or dead, is entirely coincidental.

HARPER

An Imprint of HarperCollins*Publishers*
10 East 53rd Street
New York, New York 10022-5299

First Harper paperback printing: October 2007

HarperCollins® and Harper® are registered trademarks of HarperCollins Publishers.

Printed in the United States of America

Visit Harper paperbacks on the World Wide Web at
www.harpercollins.com

10 9 8 7 6 5 4 3 2 1

for H. M.,
who is the Old Man . . .

ME TANNER,
YOU JANE

Chapter 1

I **have never liked** funerals. I can appreciate the advantages of conventionalizing one's relationship with Death, but this appreciation has never advanced beyond the level of pure theory. I do not like to view the televised funerals of assassinees, nor do I enjoy attending the last rites of friends and relatives. When I am introduced to an undertaker I categorize him at once as a sanctimonious money-grubbing necrophiliac. I realize this is an unfair generalization. I don't care.

As far as I was concerned, this particular funeral was the worst of a bad lot. And this for purely subjective reasons: I had to get to the funeral parlor early and stay until the bitter end. I was going to miss the party afterward. And on top of everything else, the poor son of a bitch in the rosewood casket was the one person on earth I cared most for. All of this, added to my personal distaste for such ceremonies, made me sincerely wish I was miles from there.

But that was out of the question. They couldn't have the show without me, because that was me, see, in that box there. We were gathered together in Klaus Hammacher's funeral home in Griggstown, the capital city of Modonoland, for the last rites and burial of Evan

Michael Tanner. And I'm him, or he's me. Or what you will.

Eccchhh.

"We will bury you," Armand Karp had said. Armand was a wrinkled Belgian Jew who had transplanted himself in Griggstown soil thirty years ago. Since then he had both flourished and withered, growing ever fatter in the trunk and ever thinner in the arms and legs and neck. "We will bury you," he had said, eyes twinkling in his wizened face, and the phrase was neither as menacing nor as metaphorical as it had been when Nikita said it.

"There are things to be considered," he explained. He was speaking English, and had this sort of trouble with suffixes. He was fluent in French and Flemish and Yiddish and German, and better than good in Dutch and Hebrew, and we could have talked in any of these, but there were others in that basement room and English was the one language common to us all. Thus there were things to be considered. "To continue. You are under house arrest. You are identificated with the Movement for Moderation in Modonoland. You are suspected for agitatement and making trouble. And you must removalize yourself from this house, which is my house—"

"Which is that our house is your house, Evan," Karp's wife said.

"This goes without statement, Evan. You know this. But facts must be faced. You must removalize yourself from here, you must get out of Griggstown altogether, and from there you have activation of your own to be done upon. So what is to be done upon? We will bury you, obviously, and then we will dig you up again, and then you will go on your merriment way."

"Uh," I said.

"We might announce the death this evening," Dawson Dowling said. He was very tall and very black and either an industrial chemist or a chemical industrialist. Armand had told me, the title coming out something like chemistical industrialization, so there was no way to be certain. "The burial might take place on Friday."

"Uh," I said.

"Of course Hammacher would do the service," Eyck said. He was Dutch and did something with diamonds.

"He overcharges," someone observed.

"But he can be trusted. And what is to charge? The coffin will be returned to him, and there is to be no embalming, no plastic surgery, no—"

"Uh," I said. "I just thought of something."

They looked at me and I at them. There were about twenty of them gathered in that damp basement room, sitting on card chairs and orange crates, smoking large fat pipes and thin black cigars. Half of them were black and half of them were white and one of them was Plum, and they represented the hard core of the MMM, which in Griggstown had nothing to do with Scotch tape and everything to do with revolution, and they wanted to bury me.

"The something I thought of," I told them, "is that we could do all of this more directly. By skipping the whole burial process, that is. I could just removalize myself from here"—Karp's affliction was contagious—"and, uh, get out of town. Just like that."

"But you are under house arrest, Evan."

"We're all under house arrest," I said. "All but what? Two or three of us? Yet you all managed to sneak out and come here tonight. For me, house arrest means that there's a clown out front leaning up against a palm tree and looking at the front door every few hours. But nobody's watching the back door, and—"

I broke off. No one was saying anything, but they were all looking at me very sadly.

Plum said, "You do not understand, Evan."

"What don't I understand?"

"About house arrest." Plum was fifteen years old, slim-hipped and wide-eyed and the color of blond motel furniture. Her father had been a Welsh soldier of fortune and her mother had been, and still was, a native of Griggstown, and Pelham "Plum" Jenkins was a product of their ephemeral alliance. This sort of thing didn't happen in Modonoland, where everything was black and white and there were no shades of yellow. Plum was nevertheless about as sane as anyone in the MMM.

I asked her to explain.

"We are all under house arrest," she said, "and we all snuck out. But we can all sneak back in again and no one will know the difference, or if they do they won't be too shirty about it. But if you snuck out, you wouldn't come back and they would all know about it. And also you are a foreigner and there is talk about you being a spy and a secret agent and all sorts of things, and this would bother them. It would be all right for you, but we would be in trouble."

"Oh," I said.

"And with the political situation the way it is, and the executions scheduled—"

I nodded. I understood.

"So," Karp said, "if you are voluntary—"

"What the hell," I said. "I don't mind. It's my funeral."

And now I lay in my coffin, and a beautiful thing it was, all oiled rosewood with ornamental carving and brass hardware. And what a beautiful thing I was, for that matter, with cotton pads under my lips and rouge on my cheeks and my nails manicured and my hands powdered and a single African lily clasped in them. Klaus Hammacher had done everything but embalm me (and would have done that if he could), and his careful application of the very techniques which allegedly brought life to the features of the dead made me look like the entrée at a ghouls' banquet. My cheeks looked waxen, my hair looked like a wig, and my future looked dim.

"He looks so natural," someone said. "So lifelike."

"Hammacher does beautiful work."

"Oh, he's an artist. When my mother died, God rest her soul, he took years off her. She hadn't looked so good—"

They drifted off and I tuned them out. The open-casket bit was something I've always considered tasteless to begin with, and now it was an abomination. But everyone had insisted on it, from the doctor who had doctored a death certificate to Hammacher himself. The argument was that agents of the white supremacist junta would surely attend the funeral, and they would require more than the sight of a closed casket to assure themselves that the notorious American agent was truly and properly dead.

Actually I was as close to dead as I could manage. There's this yogic relaxation technique that I do when I want to rest, involving a regimen of tensing and relaxing all one's muscles and making one's mind as blank as possible and slowing various bodily functions, and I was doing this. I kept my breathing as shallow as I could, and a rig Hammacher had contrived kept my suit jacket and shirt front in place and concealed any rise and fall of my chest.

"Such a young man! The prime of life. What did he die of?"

"They said encephalitis—"

Encephalitis. Sleeping sickness. The corpse considered this and had trouble keeping a straight face. It was indeed to laugh.

And a woman's voice, slow, halting, thickly accented: "You know, he doesn't look dead. To look at him, you would think he was alive. You would look at him and you would say, hoo, he ain't dead, hoo, he's only sleeping."

Hoo.

Well, you get the idea. It went on from there, and I suppose the service was shorter than usual, and I know it seemed longer. Tom Sawyer, I seem to remember, had a grand time at his own funeral. *De gustibus* and all that. I had a rotten time myself.

When the service ended, Hammacher and his assistant closed the casket and nailed down the lid, and it was like all those dim dark nightmares. There were air holes in the box, and I had rehearsed this part of it before and knew it was possible to breathe, but when they hammered those nails home the air inside there suddenly seemed inadequate in the extreme.

Then six good men and true bore my pall to the rickety old hearse. They might have carried me more carefully. The hearse bounced and jounced over a terrible old road out to the cemetery, and there was a mercifully short graveside service that I, mercifully, couldn't hear very clearly through the coffin lid. And then there was a hell of a wrench and the coffin was abruptly lowered six feet to the bottom of the fresh grave. I suppose it was imagination at work, but at once the air in the box seemed to turn cold and clammy and tainted with the odors of embalming fluid and formaldehyde.

Then a pause, during which I suppose the mourners and curiosity seekers went away, and then conversation I could not make out, and then the first horrible thud of the first horrible shovelful of earth on the coffin lid.

This was the part I hated. The funeral was bad enough, and the coffin and the grave were worse, but the idea of having them fill in the hole was too much. Since I was going to be disinterred in an hour or two, I couldn't see why they had to fill in the hole and then dig it up all over again. It reminded me of a WPA project and made about as much sense.

But there was no way around it. Three alcoholics had the grave-digging concession in Griggstown, and it was inconceivable that anyone else could play their part in the drama, and it was at least as inconceivable that they be trusted with the knowledge of my undead state. In the interests of security they had to be allowed to fill in the hole, and later on some of the MMM comrades would unfill it, and rescue me, and fill it again, and that, presumably, would be that.

They were a long time filling that grave, and if I hadn't been breathing very shallowly, very economically, I might have run out of air before they ran out of dirt. But finally they seemed to be done, and I took the six foot-long lengths of aluminum tubing from beside me, and I dislodged the little inch-wide plug in the coffin lid, and I pushed the lengths of tubing up through the lid and through the earth above it, fitting them through one by one, screwing them together, and eventually creating a breathing tube reaching just to the surface.

This process probably sounds incredibly awkward. It should, because it was. I had practiced it over and over beforehand, and I had become as good at it as it was possible to be, and it was still awkward. But it worked. It honestly worked. The end of my breathing tube broke the earth's surface, and I blew the dirt out of its tip, and I drew air through it. It was damp air, warm air, muggy air, but it was very goddamned fresh air compared to the air in the box with me, and I took deep breaths in and out, in and out, in and out, and began waiting for them to dig me up.

It was quite a wait.

Well, I had known it would take a while. The burial had taken place as late in the afternoon as we had been able to arrange it, but the unburial could not possibly occur before nightfall. Cover of darkness and all, and absence of visitors to other graves. I was able to get my eye to the breathing tube, and while there was predictably little to see through six feet of narrowing tubing, I could tell that it was light up there at first, and later on I looked and it seemed to be a little darker, and later still I looked and it was black. That was as close as I came to knowing what time it was. I didn't have a watch. I could have been buried with a watch—people get buried with watches all the time—but I hadn't been wearing a watch to begin with, and it had never occurred to me to get one to be buried in.

"The important consideration is to relax," Karp had said. "You'll have some cheese, maybe a sandwich. Also a bottle of water. You will breathe through the tube. All the comforts. It will be dark. You could have a flashlight if you wanted to read, or for passing the time you could just stretch out and have a sleep."

There was cheese concealed by my left foot and a ham sandwich by my right foot and a tiny flashlight in one pocket and a book in another pocket and a half pint of water between my knees. None of them seemed worth the trouble of trying to reach them. There just wasn't that much mobility in the box, and I just wasn't in the mood for eating or drinking or reading.

As for sleeping—

Hoo. Sleeping sickness. He ain't dead, he's only sleeping. You could just stretch out and have a sleep.

Hoo.

I haven't slept since Korea. I was in the Army, and the Army was in Korea, and a North Korean shell exploded closer to me than I would have preferred it, and one of the fragments of the shell went into my head, which is no pleasanter than it sounds. Somewhere inside there it found its way into the sleep center.

The sleep center is a clever little rascal that makes you sleep. Doctors don't know much about it, except that this is what it does, and that everyone has one. Except me, that is. I don't have one, and consequently I don't sleep.

This is mostly good, I think. I get a disability pension from the government in the amount of $112 a month. (I don't know where they got the figure, or how.) And I have time to do all the things that people don't have time for. Like learning languages (once you've learned eight or ten, the rest get very easy) and getting involved with political causes (like the return of the House of Stuart to the English throne, or the restoration of Cilician Armenia, or the propagation of the beliefs of the Flat Earth Society, or the destruction of the white supremacist government of Modonoland, or, oh, lots of things). When you stop to think about it, eight hours out of twenty-four is a lot of time to waste on nothing more interesting than unconsciousness.

But there are times when being awake is not that much of a joy. There are times, in truth, when the raveled sleeve of care could use a little knitting up.

This was one of them.

And it went on and on and on, until I felt that time simply could not be passing this slowly. Obviously I had lost my sense of time. I had also lost my sense of humor, and I only wished I could lose my sense of smell in the bargain, because the air holes in the casket facilitated a certain amount of seepage, and, not to put too fine a point on it, that casket was no bed of roses.

Until finally I heard footsteps, heard them very clearly through all that earth, and they came closer and closer, just a single set of footsteps, and a voice shouted out my name.

"Evan!"

My skull started vibrating. The earth was a much better conductor of sound than I would have guessed. It was like a loud noise under water, only worse. I called back through the breathing tube, saying things like *"Not so loud."*

More gently: "Evan?" It was Plum. "It's Plum," she said, unnecessarily. "I'm here," she said, pointlessly. "Plum," she said, redundantly.

"Where is everybody?"

"They're not here. Evan—"

"What time is it?"

"A little after eleven. Evan—"

"Eleven! What the hell happened? Where did everybody go? Why am I still here?"

Silence.

"Plum?"

Sounds of a girl crying.

"Plum—"

"You won't let me tell you."

"I'm sorry."

"They can't, they aren't, they can't come for you."

"They what?"

"The wake," she said, and sobbed again. "There was a wake. For you. Your wake. A party after the funeral. At Armand's house. A wake."

"So?"

"There was a lot to drink. There was, oh, there were other people besides the MMM people, and it had to be authentic, you know, and some people got very drunk. Because of having too much to drink."

"That'll do it."

"Pardon me?"

"Nothing. Go on. What happened?"

"I guess it was very noisy there."

"Oh."

"Singing and carrying on, you know."

"Oh."

"And someone—you know Armand doesn't get on with his neighbors—and some neighbor called the police, and you know how the police feel about us all. And they came, and of course there were black and white together at the party, as a matter of fact that was the song they were all singing, *Black and White Together, We Shall Not Be Moved,* and the police came in."

"Oh, God."

"And arrested everybody."

"Oh, shit."

"And they can't come, because they're all in jail, all but me, and I don't even know where to get a shovel, and I don't think, I don't, I don't—"

She began crying again.

It was just as well. If she hadn't cried I might have. Instead I set about reassuring her.

"Calm yourself down," I told her. "There's nothing to worry about. I'm comfortable here. In a sense. Uh. And I have food, see, and enough water, and I can breathe my silly head off through this tube, and it's not that bad, really it's not. If I have to wait here for a day, or even two days, I can manage it."

She cried a little more, and then she calmed down, and I talked some more, and she talked a little, and I thought about things and started scrunching around for the bottle of water and the sandwich, and then the loudest noise in the history of sound happened.

I asked what it was.

"Thunder."

"Oh," I said.

"It looked like rain all day."

"Oh."

And when the first drops of water trickled through my breathing tube, I realized exactly what was going to happen.

I was going to drown.

I closed my eyes, and I gritted my teeth, and I composed my spirits, and I waited for my whole life to flash through my mind. But it didn't work quite that way. Not my whole life. Just the past couple of weeks—

Chapter 2

Leaving New York in the middle of February was not exactly like the expulsion from Eden. There was one similarity—I was driven, by third-string devils if not by an angel. And there was one major difference—I was glad to go.

For a lot of reasons.

The weather, for instance. I live in four and a half rooms five flights above sea level on 107th Street west of Broadway, and the weather there is rather nice for about nineteen days in the year, and none of those days come in February. It had been a mild winter up until then, a deceptively mild winter, and it even seemed as though the winter was coming to an end, and then the groundhog did or didn't see his shadow, whichever is the bad omen. I can never keep it straight. The groundhog supplied the bad news, and the heavens supplied the snow, and the municipal government demonstrated a blend of foresight and preparedness reminiscent of Pearl Harbor Day. The snow came down white, turned gray as it passed my windows, and blackened on the streets and sidewalks, where it lay waiting, like all the rest of us, for warmer times.

"Snow," Minna called out when it first began falling. "Can I go out and play in it, Evan?"

"Do you really think you want to?"

"Oh, it's so beautiful," she chirped, and ran down the stairs.

She came back a few minutes later. "It's all dirty," she said. "What happened to it?"

"New York happened to it," I told her.

"Well, I don't like it," she said. "I'll sit on your lap and we can read *Alice*, Evan."

She sat on my lap and I let her do the reading. She picked out a German edition of *Through the Looking-Glass,* Hans Gebhardt's translation, and read the chapter about Humpty Dumpty, which works beautifully in German. I couldn't pay too much attention to the words. She squirmed around a little on my lap, and I kept hearing re-runs of a conversation I'd had a few weeks earlier with an old love.

"You'll have to do something about Minna, Evan."

"Minna? What's wrong with Minna?"

"The whole situation. It's not as if she were your daughter, you know. She's just a child who lives with you. And she won't be a child forever."

"Well, only Peter Pan—"

"She's growing up already, you know."

"Huh?"

"She is, Evan. How old is she? Ten?"

"Nine. She's not exactly eligible for Social Security yet."

"Nine years old. You know, children are growing up a lot faster these days, Evan."

"You sound like a Sunday supplement."

"I mean sexually. Do you know that puberty begins

*an average of three years earlier than it did a century
ago? Do you realize what that means?"*

"For a belly dancer, you've got a dirty mind."

"I'm serious."

"I know."

*"You keep her out of school and you teach her lan-
guages and you take her to the zoo and drag her around
to nut group meetings and it's all very sweet and cute,
and one of these days you're going to take a good look
at her and not be able to decide whether to change her
diaper or take her to bed, and when that happens—"*

"You're out of your mind."

"If you had children of your own—"

"I do. In Macedonia. Two boys. Todor and Benno."

*"Oh, Evan, don't you see how chaotic this is? Don't
you see—"*

"Let's talk about something else, Kitty."

And we talked about something else, something more
cheerful, like an earthquake or a tidal wave or an epidemic.
Now, while Minna read Humpfe Dumpfe's speech about
a word meaning precisely what one wants it to mean, neither more nor less, I thought about Minna and puberty,
visualizing the little golden-haired angel against a background montage of Tampax and Clearasil ads.

I had found her three years before in a windowless
basement in Lithuania. She was the sole living descen-
dant of Mindaugas, the first and last king of independent
Lithuania, and someday, according to her guardians,
she would be queen. I took her out of that basement
and brought her home with me, and ever since then my
life had never been the same.

She would reach puberty at about the same time that I reached forty. Both prospects were unendurably upsetting. I started to put my arm around her, and for the first time I wondered if maybe I shouldn't put my arm around her, and I winced, and she read about Alice while I thought first of Lewis Carroll and then of Vladimir Nabokov and finally of auto-defenestration.

The next night I trudged to the subway and went down to the New Life restaurant on West 28th, where Katin Bazerian dances, wearing the name Alexandra the Great and comfortingly little else. I caught the last set. When it was over Kitty came to my table and we did in a bottle of rhodytis. We listened to bouzouki music and didn't talk much.

Eventually I said, "Get your coat and come home with me."

"I don't know."

"What's to know? We're nice people and we love each other and we should go home together."

"Oh? We love each other?"

"We always have."

"You drift from girl to girl, Evan, like a bee from flower to flower. Like a dog from hydrant to hydrant. Evan, I think there are healthier things in this world than our cockamamie relationship."

It is always bad when girls talk about relationships. They shouldn't be allowed to use the word.

"I always thought you liked our relationship," I said.

"Oh, I do. Oh, shit, everything's rotten." And she looked at the floor, and I watched the wine evaporate in my glass, and she looked up and said, "He wants to marry me."

"Who does?"

"A . . . a fellow. You don't know him. He's a nice boy, he works steady. He's an assistant cook at Gregorio's on the next block and he plans to be a chef in a few years and he loves me and we talk to each other, you know, and we are good together, you know, I mean bed, we're good together—"

I wanted something with more authority than rhodytis. Something like heroin, for instance.

"Evan, when a woman is thirty she can frankly forget the whole thing, and I am halfway to being thirty."

"You're fifteen?"

"I'm twenty-five."

"That's halfway to—"

"Between twenty and thirty it's halfway."

"Oh."

"I mean, this life is fine up to a point, but at a certain point a woman is ready to settle down. It's a human thing, to want to settle down."

"I know."

"I'm only human."

"Uh-huh. What did you tell him?"

"That I didn't know. That I had to think."

"What are you going to tell him?"

"I'm not sure." She was silent for a few moments. "You know," she said, her voice softer, "it's a funny thing, a proposal of marriage. A very strange thing. I have been proposed to before but it was never something to take very seriously, or at least I didn't, you know, on account of not being ready to. To be serious, I mean. But it is a funny thing. It makes you feel very good, you know, that someone would ask you to marry him."

"Sure."

"I always wondered, you know, if you would some-day ask me to, uh, to marry you. And how I would feel. You know."

"Er."

"I think about it occasionally, because you're right, we do love each other. But I know you've never wanted to get married so I never pushed anything. But when this fellow asked me, oh, I thought how I had two minds about it, and I asked myself how would I feel if it had been you proposing instead of this fellow, and I knew I would be just of one mind. That I would want to marry you. And make a home with you, with you and Minna, sort of a ready-made family almost, and, oh, this is just what went through my mind and I shouldn't have said anything to you but I couldn't help it—"

Her voice just trailed off, as if fading in the distance.

"I'd better get my coat and go home now, Evan," she said a little later. "To Brooklyn."

"I'll take you."

"No, please, I'll just get in a cab."

"I'll put you in a cab."

"Well, if you want."

I flagged a cab on Seventh Avenue. I held the door for her and said, "Look, I don't want you to marry this cook. But I can't tell you not to because—"

"There's nothing to explain."

"I suddenly find my life completely fragmented, and up until a little while ago it had seemed very together. I have things to think about."

"I know, Evan."

I took the subway home. I missed my stop and had to walk all the way back from 116th Street. When I got home I drank a lot, but it didn't do any good.

That night was followed by two more damp and dreary days, and the best that could be said for them was that they were generally uneventful. I read my mail, I answered my telephone, I grunted at Minna, and now and then I went around the corner to the liquor store. The second day I got a phone call from a girl who was a friend of a friend and who had just gotten into town and needed a place to stay, and ordinarily she would have been a perfectly satisfactory girl, and ordinarily one girl is the world's best way to get over another girl, but this was not an ordinary time. My dilemma was hornier than I was. I found a place for the girl to stay, and I took her there and left her there. She seemed surprised.

On the morning of the third day I went around the corner for breakfast. I sat at the counter and had scrambled eggs and home fries and as much coffee as possible. There were a few tables of Columbia students in the back, but I was the only diner at the counter, just me and eight empty stools. I was working on a fourth cup of coffee when the door opened and the Sikh came in. He was six and a half feet tall, with the final six inches consisting of turban. He had a full black beard, a bronze face, baggy pantaloons, and bore a scimitar in a tooled brass sheath. I looked at him and decided I was hallucinating. He looked both ways like a conscientious child at a crosswalk, and then he strode to the counter and took the stool next to mine.

The waitress was a solid stolid lady whom nothing surprises. She moved to take his order. The Sikh extended his lower jaw slightly, retrieved it, smiled carefully, and said that he would like an extra dry martini, made with Bombay gin, straight up, with just a twist of lemon peel. The waitress shook her head.

"I am a guest in your nation," the Sikh said.

I had a fair idea what this was going to be all about. One develops a feel over the years. I turned to the Sikh and told him the place didn't serve liquor.

"Ah," he said. "My apologies, good madam. Apple pie and coffee, if you please."

She brought it, served him, and went away, all without changing expression. I waited. After ingesting the final bite of apple pie and swallowing the final sip of coffee, the Sikh lowered his head and said, "Twelve-fifteen, Hotel Garrand, Room 1304, Mr. Cuttlefish. Godspeed!"

And left.

Of course it was the Chief. Who else sends a costumed Sikh to drink martinis in a Broadway diner? Who else employs couriers who wed the inconspicuousness of the Eiffel Tower to the subtlety of a nuclear warhead?

So I went to the Hotel Garrand, and shortly after

twelve I got into the elevator. The Garrand, it turned out, had no thirteenth floor. I went back to the desk and asked about Mr. Cuttlefish, who turned out to be in Room 1403. Well, no one's perfect.

He opened the door just as I knocked on it. "Tanner," he said, beaming at me. "Come in, come in. A drink?"

He poured scotch for both of us, gave me a glass, narrowed his eyes, frowned.

"You knew Joe Klausner, didn't you?" I had. "Then you'll join me in drinking a toast to his memory."

"What happened?"

"In Berlin. Stuffed into the engine compartment of his own Volkswagen. The engine had been removed. He'd been onto something and evidently they got onto him. Piano wire around his neck. Eyeballs all popped out of his head. Face all bloody purple. I'm not being British about it. That was the color, bloody purple."

I made a sound mixing sympathy with nausea. The Chief turned, looked out across the room. Then he turned to face me again. "To Klausner," he said.

"To Klausner."

We drank.

I have never been able to decide whether the Chief is particularly intelligent or particularly stupid. Most of the time I suspect he's merely mediocre, but it's impossible to be sure. He runs a nameless intelligence agency that is so secret that its own agents don't know how to get in touch with it. His employees operate on their own initiative, establish their own contacts, pull their own strings, and ultimately cut their own throats. You don't have to write out reports when you work for him, nor do you have to worry about any of the usual bureaucratic claptrap. You just go out and do the job.

The Chief thinks I'm one of his best men. He got this idea about four years ago and I've never seen fit to disabuse him of the notion. Every once in a while he finds some dumb way to get in touch with me and shoves some assignment at me, and every once in a while I can't find a way to avoid the assignment, so maybe I work for him and maybe I don't. It's hard to be certain. The thing of it is that I'm on so many subversive lists as it is, with the FBI tapping my phone and the CIA reading my mail (or else it's the other way around), that I figure I need all the help I can get.

"Joe Klausner," he said. "My boys are on their own, Tanner, but I would have helped Joe if I could have. But all at once he was dead. Just like that." He walked to the window, looked out of it. "I didn't even know he was in Berlin. I thought he was in St. Paul, Minnesota. Then there was a call from Berlin—"

He filled his glass. "You don't know Sam Bowman," he said.

"No."

"It may be too late. Just as it was too late with Joe. But there's a chance, you know."

He drained his glass. He seems to drink all the time but never seems affected by it. Either I have never seen him drunk or I have never seen him sober.

"Ah, Tanner," he said heavily. "I don't suppose you've so much as heard of Modonoland, now have you?"

"Yes."

"Didn't think so," he said. "Most people—you have?"

"Yes."

He said that was marvelous and would save a great deal of time. I don't know what time it saved, exactly, because he was primed to deliver a certain speech and he couldn't alter his programing. "A few thousand square miles in West Africa. A British Protectorate since Versailles. German before that, but a mixed settlement of Germans and Belgians and English and Dutch. Given its independence a couple of years ago. Retained Commonwealth status. Government seesawed for a while. Then a strong man came along."

"Knanda Ndoro," I said.

"Kuhnanda Nuhdoro," he said, adding a couple of syllables. "The Glorious Retriever, he called himself. Sounds like something that might be useful for hunting waterfowl." He chuckled deeply. "Typical African dictator at first. Went about building grand marble mausoleums and calling them government office buildings and cultural centers and such. Scattered statues of his beautiful self wherever two streets intersected. Which didn't happen too often, Modonoland being on the primitive side. Did the usual, you know. Had himself a harem, lopped off the heads of the loyal opposition, usual sort of thing.

"And then a couple of years ago the Retriever did something rather extraordinary. The trouble with Modonoland, as with most of these damned countries, is that most of it is just wasted. Just space with jungles and lions and tigers and what-not. And when they try doing something about it, why they only plant some crop that someone else grows better and cheaper, and get touchy if the U.S. doesn't buy it from them. Ndoro, now, struck off on a new path. You wouldn't guess what he grew."

"Opium," I said heavily.

"Opium," he said lightly. He didn't seem to have heard me. "Opium. Planted half of Modonoland with opium, giving himself a big cash crop and cutting the underpinnings from the Red Chinese opium trade in the bargain. A first-class development, you know. We couldn't have been happier."

I studied the floor. Stains made a pattern on the carpet, and I wondered if they could be augered, like birds' entrails.

"And then not too long ago there was an uprising," he went on. "It was a long while in the wind, and for a time it looked as though some sort of lefties were going to move in. Group called the Movement for Moderation in Modonoland. Batch of political amateurs, but well-financed. Moscow gold, I suspect. Or Peking, more likely.

"They had Ndoro's government shaking like a leaf, and we were all a bit worried. Unknowns are a danger, you know. Better to stay with the old status quo. At the same time, we determined that Ndoro had to fall. There are times, you know, when it's strategically unwise to try propping up an unpopular regime. Can't always be done."

I murmured something about Saigon. His eyes met mine for an instant, then withdrew.

"But we did have a bit of luck, Tanner. We thought

about reinforcing Ndoro, and we rejected that, and then we found out that there were some white men who thought they ought to have a crack at running Modono-land on their own hook. Old line colonialists out of the same mold as the Rhodesians. Oh, I suppose you might call them reactionaries or white supremacists or something of the sort—"

"Or fascists," I suggested.

"—but there's no denying that they weren't the sort to rock the old boat. Kept the opium trade flourishing, for one thing—and the MMM fanatics had intended to put a stop to it. And kept things more or less on an even keel foreign policywise. There's some trouble with England, some question about the Commonwealth status, but all in all they're the sort of people we can support. We may not boast about them, but we're glad to see them around."

I didn't say anything.

"Now here's where it gets a little sticky, Tanner. On the one hand, we gave these white supremacist fellows a little support. Our Boy Scout chums were in on that, and kept it a sight quieter than their usual sort of thing." He grinned nastily. "They've been a little less boisterous since the Bay of Pigs, haven't they? As I say, they handled that end. But at the same time, we had to do something for this Retriever fellow, this Knanda Ndoro. So I sent a man in to let Ndoro know as much of the score as we wanted to tell him, and to help him get out with his skin intact when the time came. I had a feeling Ndoro wasn't too keen on white men, what with all the white men trying to chuck him out, so I sent my best black agent."

"And that was Sam Bowman?"

"Samuel Lonestar Bowman," he said. "A former burglar, heroin addict, and strong-arm man. Became a Black Muslim in jail. Broke with Elijah Muhammad about the same time Malcolm X did. Organized for the Black Panthers on the West Coast. Shot a policeman in a gun battle, possibly in self-defense, possibly not. Decided to get out of the country. Went to a friend of his, who happened to be a lad of mine. We got him out and added him to the payroll, and he's been damned good ever since. He went into Modonoland to help Ndoro pack up the royal treasury and get out. Got to him in the nick of time, and the two of them left the back door of the palace while a white mob kicked in the front door. It was about that close, according to the reports I've seen.

"Then the two of them headed inland. Two men with a fortune in jewels and hard currencies. They disappeared into the bloody jungle, and they haven't come out of it yet, and it does not look good, Tanner. Not good at all."

"There's been no word?"

"No direct word. Rumors, though."

"Rumors?"

He hesitated. "A group of bandits, guerrillas, what have you. Operating deep in the Modonoland interior. One never knows what's to be believed, but they seem to be a band of black religious fanatics led by a . . . this is slightly fantastic, Tanner."

I waited.

"Led by a blond-haired white-skinned jungle goddess of some sort."

"Is that so," I said.

"Named Sheena."

"Sheena, Queen of the Jungle," I said.

"You've heard of her?"

"No."

"Then—"

"It's nothing. I'm sorry."

"Er," he said. "Well, rumors would suggest that this Sheena person has captured Ndoro and Bowman. And while of course she may have had them killed, she doesn't seem to kill blacks, not as a general rule. So there's a chance that they're alive, and that they could be gotten to and brought out alive, and—"

"And I'm elected."

"I hate to risk you on something this speculative, Evan." He rarely called me Evan. Only when he was feeling very paternal or when he was conning me. "But this would be a good one to pull off. The situation in Modonoland is troubled. We may yet find a political use for the Retriever. And as for Bowman, well, he's been a tremendous asset to us. Actually, to get down to cases, he's our best black operative. In fact—"

"Yes?"

"Well, he's our only black operative."

"Oh."

"Not because of policy. It's just happened that way. I had been wanting to take on some Negroes for ages. It was still all right to call them Negroes then. In fact when I first wanted to hire one, they preferred to be called colored. I wonder what the word will be after black? I shouldn't be surprised if things come full circle, don't you know, and they insist upon calling themselves niggers." He replenished his scotch, and mine as well. "Hmm," he said. "Point is, we don't run recruiting ads, do we? So with one thing and another, well, we never did take one on. Until Sam Bowman came along, and he couldn't have been better, you know, and now it looks as though I've lost him. There are times, Evan, when a black operative has a distinct advantage."

"At night," I suggested.

He didn't appear to have heard me. "In the Modonoland affair, for example. And in other situations as well. God alone knows where I would get another one." He sipped his drink. "So I'm asking you to go to an unholy haystack and search for a needle that very probably isn't there. I'd prefer to paint you a rosier picture, but in all conscience—well. What do you say?"

"I'll go."

"You will?"

I nodded.

And so I went to the post office and told them to hold my mail and went to Brooklyn and boarded Minna with Kitty and her grandmother and tied my money belt around my waist and put my passport in my pocket and went away. I caught a Sabena flight to Brussels and another Sabena flight to Leopoldville. I flew Central African Airways into Nairobi, where I knew some people. They arranged for the necessary papers, and I got a slot as a deck hand on a Portuguese freighter that got me to Griggstown in five days.

It would have been easier to fly directly to

Griggstown. Almost directly, anyway, via either Cape-town or Salisbury. But I felt it wouldn't be a good idea to let the Modonoland officials see my name on an incoming passenger list.

Modonoland and I go back a ways.

The opium, for example. It was largely my fault that it was growing there. Once upon a time I'd been talking to Abel Vaudois, a Swiss who lives in Bangkok, and I guess I gave him the idea of growing opium in Africa, and he subsequently made the deal with Knanda Ndoro.

So I had felt responsible, and when Abel sent me a bank draft as payment for the idea, I gave a large portion of it to the MMM. And if it hadn't been for the MMM there would have been no white supremacist coup, and if it hadn't been for me I don't suppose there would have been much of an MMM, so—

Well, one thing leads to another, doesn't it? Modonoland bothered the hell out of me. I hated to read news stories from there. They all seemed personally accusing.

All of which did not quite add up to enough of a reason to pursue wild geese in that beleaguered nation. I might feel compelled to send them a check now and then, and write occasional propaganda for the cause, and give aid and comfort to any MMM comrades who came to New York. But to chase all the way over there in search of the Retriever and the black militant who had been sent to retrieve him, that was something else.

Something which would have ordinarily remained undone.

But.

But Kitty wanted to get married, and Minna was growing up, and New York was not a winter festival, and he who turns and runs away lives to run another day. And when it is January in New York it is July in Modonoland. Or, more accurately, when it is January in New York it is also January in Modonoland, since they use the same calendar we do, but January in Modonoland is a far cry from January in New York, Modonoland being in the Southern Hemisphere and their summer occurring during our winter, all of which is childishly simple to understand and maturely difficult to explain.

So I went there.

So they buried me.

Chapter 3

"**E**van? **Are you** all right?"

"No."

"It's raining."

"It certainly is."

"Are you all right?"

"No."

"Because for a moment I was talking to you and you didn't answer me."

"I was thinking about something."

"Oh. Are you all right?"

She was evidently going to keep on asking until I said yes. So I said yes. And as I did so, the water stopped dripping through the tube. But it was still raining. I could hear it. I put my lips to the tube and sipped air.

"It's still raining," I said.

"It's pouring."

"But the water's not coming through the tube."

"I'm sort of hunched over it, Evan."

"Oh."

"Is that bad?"

"No," I said. "Don't move. Or I'll drown."

"Oh."

"I may drown anyway. There's a certain amount of

seepage going on in here. I don't know who manu-
factured this casket, but the quality control isn't all it
should be. Plum?"

"What?"

"I sort of have to get out of here."

"Oh, Evan—"

I put my hands against the lid of the coffin, took
a breath, composed myself, and with all my strength
pushed at the coffin lid.

Nothing whatsoever happened.

"It's all nailed and bolted together," I said. "If I could
just take the damned thing apart."

"Do you have any tools down there?"

"A book, a ham sandwich, a money belt—you'd
think I could *buy* my way out, for Christ's sake. A
flashlight—just a second, maybe I can get a hold of
that flashlight."

I squirmed around and managed to get my hand in
my pocket. It was the wrong pocket. I squirmed some
more and found the right pocket and got the flashlight
out. I switched it on. It was a tiny little thing but it was
blinding in there. I blinked at the light for a few seconds, then played it around the interior of the casket.
There were all sorts of hinges and clasps and things,
and none of them looked as though my fingernails
would have much effect on them.

"You have the light, Evan? Will you be able to get
out now?"

"I don't see how," I said. "I would need, oh, a screwdriver and a knife and a saw and God knows what
else."

"I have them."

"Sure."

"I'll give them to you."

"Sure, Plum. That's wonderful."

"What is the matter, Evan?"

I said, "Once upon a time there were two brothers, and they both went out and bought horses. And they had to figure out how to tell the horses apart. They counted their hoofs, but both horses had the same number. They painted a big X on one, but the rain washed it off. Finally they measured them, and lo and behold they had a sure-fire way to tell them apart, because the black horse was two inches shorter than the white horse."

"But if one was black and the other white—"

"That's the point, Plum."

"I don't understand why you raise the question of color at a time like this."

I closed my eyes for a few seconds. Then I said, "No, you don't understand, Plum. It's the same as telling the horses apart. If you could pass me a knife and a screwdriver and a saw and I don't know what else, there would be a space big enough to crawl through, and I wouldn't need the tools to begin with. Like the horses."

"Look out, Evan."

"Huh?"

Look out for what, I wondered. And, in answer to my question, something plummeted through the breathing tube and hit me in the mouth. I made the appropriate noise and Plum said that she was sorry but that she had warned me. This was true enough.

I found the thing that had hit me. I said, "Oh."

"You see, Evan?"

"It's one of those knives," I said.

"Yes."

"One of those knives with a hundred blades in it."

"Sixteen blades, I think."

"They sell them in those little schlock shops on Times Square. Swiss Navy knives or something—"

"Swiss Army pocketknives."

"That's it." I began opening the knife. There was a nail file, a tiny pair of scissors, a thing for making holes in your belt—

"It was my father's," Plum said. "It was his legacy to me. I always carry it."

"I didn't know he was in the Swiss Army."

"He was in every army at one time or another. My mother told me this. My father was a brave mad Welshman with wild eyes and the soul of a poet."

I kept on opening the knife. A can opener, a cap lifter, a saw, a couple of cutting blades, a chisel—

"You carry this around all the time?"

"Always, Evan."

"I'm glad you do, but why?"

"For protection, Evan. A girl my age—"

"Protection?"

"Yes."

"By the time you found the right blade, and got it open, you wouldn't have much left to protect."

She began to giggle. I opened a few more blades and found one that was designed, among other things, for unscrewing screws. I think it also told time, recited the Lord's Prayer in three languages, and kept bridge scores. Plum went on giggling, and I started doing things to the screws that held the hinges that connected the coffin lid to the coffin.

None of this was very easy. Coffins, after all, are designed with the law of inertia in mind; their dimensions are founded on the assumption that bodies at rest tend to remain at rest. There is thus rather little room to move around in.

But the human body contends throughout life with the task of fitting itself into and through impossibly narrow apertures. But for this propensity, we would none of us be born. Or, come to think of it, conceived.

I did everything I could think of to the coffin, and while I worked Plum prattled on and on about her father and her mother and the problems of being neither black nor white in a country where everyone else was one or the other. I suspect that much of what she had to say was very interesting, but I was in no position to pay any attention to it. I was glad she was talking; it was a sort of verbal Muzak, and now and then I would grunt something at her so that she would know I was still alive.

I'm sure I didn't use all sixteen of those blades. I don't remember cutting anything with the scissors, for example, and I can't recall lifting any caps or opening any cans. But I cut and I twisted and I pried and I poked and I probed and I filed and I unscrewed and I got the hinges off on one side and worked the lid up on the other side and loosened the nails and got them out and finally, incredibly, the cover was off.

"Hey!" I said. "It's off."

There was no answer.

"The cover," I said. "It's loose. It's off, I got it off, your father's knife, it did the job. God bless the Swiss Army. We did it. Hey—"

The drums began.

They seemed to be everywhere. It was the unusual acoustics of my little *pied à terre* that was responsible for the effect, no doubt, but what an effect it was. I seemed to be hearing a drum concert on the ultimate stereo rig, one that had me completely surrounded with woofers and tweeters. Drumming pulsed up from beneath me, pounded at me from all sides, came down upon me from above. It sounded as though the very continent of Africa itself was displaying its natural sense of rhythm. There was something particularly enervating about the beat of those drums, and I think it may have been that the tempo was just a shade faster than my own heartbeat, so that I felt as though I was struggling unsuccessfully to keep up with it.

Water was once again trickling through my breathing tube. Plum had gone off somewhere, and I couldn't exactly blame her. Some idiots with drums had taken possession of the graveyard. I wanted to go off somewhere myself.

Keep calm, I urged myself. Some sort of pagan cranks were having some sort of ritual in the cemetery. Swinging dead cats over their heads as a remedy for warts, perhaps. Or some equally innocent pursuit. Just a group of religious fanatics exercising their civil rites. They wouldn't stick around forever. It was raining, and before very long they would bow their heads for the benediction and go back to their huts. All I had to do was wait until they went away.

If it hadn't been for the drums, I might have been able to wait them out. But I had spent too many hours watching too many movies in which Stewart Granger crouched with his arm around Eleanor Parker and she said, "What do the drums mean?" or "Why did the drums stop?" or "Do you hear the drums?" The drums always signaled the beginning of something horrible. The more I listened to them the more nervous and apprehensive I became, and I had not been precisely relaxed to begin with, and things were not getting better.

I doubled up, and sought out a new position in the coffin, and got my feet braced against the now unfastened coffin lid, and snorted like a karate master, and thrust out with both feet at once.

The lid raised up about two and a half inches.

Two more tries netted another half inch at best. That seemed to be all the play I was going to get.

Okay, I decided.

No more Mr. Nice Guy.

I kicked at one side of the coffin until it loosened up some, then pried it apart with various knife blades. I pulled it into the box with me, got it down flat, crawled over it, and shoved it over to the opposite side of the coffin. There was a space of a few inches between the edge of the coffin and earthen wall of the grave. Digging at the grave wall didn't do much good—it was hard-packed earth, untouched by the gravediggers' spades. But I managed to squeeze myself against the wall of the grave and work the coffin lid down past me and into the coffin itself. I scooped dirt from the top of the coffin lid and stuffed it into empty spaces in the coffin, and I got myself on top of the lid and put more dirt where I had been, creating new places for me to put me, creating new places to put new dirt, and so on.

What it amounted to, really, was that I was pulling the hole in after me. Swimming through loose wet mud. Of course it was impossible to see or breathe or do much of anything, and if I had stopped anywhere along the line to think about what I was doing I might have given up. There was a point somewhere along the line when the fleeting thought came to mind that perhaps, God forbid, I was going in the wrong direction. I assured myself that this line of thinking was unproductive and potentially depressing, and I kept digging and squirming and writhing, and although an earthworm probably gets more of a kick out of this sort of thing, it works just the same when a person does it.

Boomlay boomlay boomlay boom, the drums said. I wormed my way skyward, and the drums got louder, and the drummers began to chant, and my lungs sent threatening letters to my brain, and the pulse in my ears was louder than the drums, and I gave a last wriggling squirming kick and broke through the surface of the earth.

The drums stopped, and there was a long and thoughtful silence, and then everyone in Africa started screaming.

Chapter 4

It had the quality of a dream sequence in a motion picture. Everything slightly out of focus, and the action shown in a ponderous, heavy-limbed slow motion. I ascended from the grave, head, neck, shoulders, chest, all of me imperfectly coated with wet mud. And all around me in a slightly off-center circle, naked black men with paint on their cheeks and foreheads waved bleached white bones overhead, pounded their feet on the ground, rolled their eyes, and screamed.

There must have been thirty of them. Plum supplied that figure later on, and she had had time to count the house. It looked to me as though there were at least a hundred of them, and they made enough noise for a thousand.

I sort of stayed where I was. They happily did not. As if on a signal they tossed their bones into the air—the ones they had been waving about, that is. And before the bones could touch the ground, the men turned and ran screaming in all directions. The bones clattered to the ground and the men kept running and kept screaming, and their screams gradually faded in the distance.

I coughed and shrugged and said, "Well, I'll be a son of a bitch," and otherwise reassured myself that I was still there. I scrambled the rest of the way out of the hole and turned to look at it. I looked down at myself and decided that I looked like something that might logically have crawled out of a grave.

I picked up one of the abandoned bones. I decided at first that it was a human leg bone, the meat but recently gnawed off by similarly human teeth. I looked at it some more and decided it was more likely the shinbone of an ox. I was still looking at it when Plum called to me. I turned, and she was just emerging from a clump of trees.

I said, "They didn't have any drums."

She looked at me oddly.

"Drums," I insisted. "They were beating drums, it was driving me crazy. Then the drums stopped and I got out of there and I didn't see any drums. Just these things." I held up the bone. "What happened to the drums?"

"They used the bones."

"How?"

"They beat on the ground with them," she said. "Evan, we have to get out of here."

I knelt down, pounded the bone on the ground. I could have made as much noise pounding a pillow with a sponge. "There must have been more to it than that," I said.

"There were a great many of them, Evan."

"I noticed."

"And they pounded with great fervor."

I pounded with great fervor myself. I began to see how it could have sounded like drumming, especially when it was all going on over my head.

Plum was busy apologizing. "I was sorry to run off

without warning, Evan. But when I saw them coming I was frightened." I couldn't exactly blame her. "I wanted only to get away without attracting their attention. Others who have spied on their midnight rituals have been killed. I was afraid."

"Who were they, anyway?"

"The Nishanti."

"Oh."

"They are outlawed, Evan. They have always been outlawed, but with the new government the penalties are most severe. And yet the Nishanti flourish. There are more of them than ever before."

"What do they do? Besides pound bones on the ground?"

"They raise the Devil."

"I'll say they do," I said. "They raise the devil, all right. But what's the point of it all?"

"No, no, Evan. That is what they do." She gestured. "Raise the Devil. It is their belief that they can come to the cemetery at midnight after a burial, and that they can chant their chants and beat bones upon the ground, and that the Devil himself will rise up out of the new grave and wreak havoc upon the entire world, and that all who do not believe will be destroyed, while the chosen believers, the Nishanti, will be carried into the Kingdom of Eternal Life."

"The Devil Himself," I said.

"Yes. They must have thought—"

"Up popped the Devil."

"Yes. That is why they spared you, you see. And why you struck terror upon them."

"They tried to raise the Devil, and they succeeded beyond their wildest dreams, and they ran off screaming. I suppose it's always that way. I suppose the Jehovah's Witnesses will be upset when the world comes to an end. But why should they be frightened if they're the chosen believers?"

She pondered this. "Perhaps they did not truly believe," she suggested.

"Well," I said, "they do now."

We left the cemetery without encountering devils or devil raisers. The bone yard was on the northeast edge of Griggstown, and the road which led to the interior of the country began in the center of town and cut northwest from there, so we made our way through the suburban sprawl along the top of the city. The rain lasted long enough to wash most of the mud off me, then turned itself off. We were both soaked through to the bone. I walked along shivering, and Plum's teeth chattered in the chill air. One of those hidden blessings—the cold and wet kept us from realizing how hungry we were.

The suburb we walked through had no formal name. It wasn't a formal political division but was merely that part of Griggstown which had occurred during the last ten years or so. I couldn't imagine why it had bothered. It was a suburb, and there is a sameness about suburbs which transcends geographical distinctions. It could have been a suburb of London or Rio de Janeiro. It was distinguished from the Eastern European suburbs in that its houses were all painted in pastels, here a pale green one, there a pale blue one, here a pink one, there a yellow one. Behind the Curtain all the houses are gray, that very gray used for the interior of every apartment building in Manhattan. But here all the little boxes were the color of infant apparel, and all the little boxes were made of concrete block, and each had a young and spindly tree in front, and a lawn of coarse-bladed grass, and an attached garage, and a car. Every once in awhile we would see a car that wasn't a Volkswagen.

The car we stole *was* a Volkswagen. I could have saved a lot of time and trouble by stealing the first car we came to, but at the time I hadn't yet decided on auto theft. It wasn't that it hadn't occurred to me. It came immediately to mind, but seemed extreme. As things stood, we were just a couple of nuts out for a walk in the middle of the night. We were both of us under house arrest, but house arrest didn't seem to be that rigid a system in Griggstown. I was also supposed to be dead, so they had probably left off looking for me entirely.

So I figured that stealing a car would just be asking for trouble. At least it seemed that way at the time, and an hour's worth of cold wet walking reduced the arguments against stealing the car a hundredfold, and Plum began talking in that mindless thick-tongued toneless way young girls talk when they are about to fall asleep on their feet. We came to a house with two Volkswagens, one in the garage and the other parked on the street, and I took it as a sign from Providence. The man was prepared. He had a spare, a reserve Volkswagen.

He might miss the one I took, but he would not be utterly discommoded by its absence.

It was locked. I took out the Swiss Army pocketknife, examined the various blades, closed them all up, and popped the vent window with the edge of the closed knife. The glass starred. I hit it again and it shattered, and I reached in and opened the door and tucked Plum inside and climbed in after her. I located the screwdriver blade and loosened the screws on the ignition plate, and I went around back and opened the engine compartment and found a wire to yank. I picked one that looked unimportant, and it turned out later that it had something to do with the directionals. At least I think it did, because they didn't work and everything else seemed to.

I used the wire to jump the ignition terminals. The whole process made me feel like a teen-ager again. I started the car, and Plum giggled with delight, and I waited for lights to go on in the house to which the car belonged. They didn't, and I drove away. It took a few minutes to get the hang of the car. But I had driven VWs before, and there was no one around to complain if I ground the gears or oversteered.

When I had the car more or less mastered I turned to look at Plum. Her huge eyes were sometimes brown and sometimes green and sometimes in-between. Her face was dusted with freckles across the bridge of the nose and high on the cheekbones. Her face was longish, the features sharply drawn, the chin strong, the forehead broad, the mouth full. Her hair was almost blond and almost kinky and not quite either. Like the car, she took a little getting used to.

I said, "Last chance, Plum."

"No."

"You sure?"

"Yes. I can help you, you know. You are a stranger in my land, Evan. You do not know the customs of the people or their speech. The geography is foreign to you. My assistance will smooth the way for you."

"I'm not sure it will be safe for you."

"Griggstown would not be safe for me either."

"I don't see—"

"They are probably searching for me right this moment," she said. "To arrest me for helping you escape from the grave. Or for violating house arrest. Or for mmmmmfrzzz."

"Huh?" I turned again, and she was asleep.

It had never occurred to me to take her along. During our traipse through the suburbs I had mentioned something about having to get her back to her house, and it was then that she insisted on coming with me. I offered up the usual sort of objections, citing her age and her sex and the fact that Griggstown was her home and that, if she left it, she might not find it easy to return to it.

None of these arguments carried much weight. She defeated them by agreeing wholeheartedly. She admitted that she was fifteen and female, and that it would be far easier to get out of Griggstown than to get back into it. But she went on to insist that it would be less dangerous for her to come with me than not, and that Griggstown wasn't much of a home for her at all because she couldn't possibly belong in it. "I'm neither white nor black," she said. "I'm in-between. Everybody gives me a funny look. I make people nervous. White or black, I make them nervous. Even the people in the MMM. They insist it's perfectly all right for the races to intermarry and that someone like me is as good as anyone else, but they don't like to look at me. I get on their nerves."

"Where would you want to go?"

"I don't know. Once I wanted to go to Capetown. There are mixed-blood people there, the Cape Coloreds. I thought I would go there and be one of them, but they seem to have the same problem, only it's worse for them because the whole country is so involved with race. Perhaps you will take me back to America."

I wasn't sure that was the answer, but neither was sending her home again. And I couldn't really see how it would be that much more dangerous for her to come along. We would just drive up into the interior of Modonoland far enough to establish that Bowman and Knanda Ndoro were with their ancestors. If there was any sign that Ndoro's treasure still existed, maybe we would have a shot at it. If not, we would find a border and get over it and find civilization and think of someplace to go next. There would be a certain amount of adventure, but that was what we were all here for. But there shouldn't be much in the way of danger.

Ha.

Chalk it up to shock—the burial bit, the madmen with their cattle bones, the rain and the chill. Or write it off as the system's tolerance for terror; after all the various anxieties I had suffered in the past few hours, nothing as far away as the remote Modonoland hinterlands held any fear for me. Besides, I was the Corpse That Walked. You can't kill a dead man, so what was there for me to be afraid of?

I drove through the geometrical precision of suburban streets until I came to the highway running northwest out of the city. I turned obliquely into it and held the car at a steady eighty kilometers an hour. Almost at once the suburban pattern thinned out and gave way to stretches of open farmland with houses few and far between. It began raining again. I hoped I hadn't ripped out the wiper system. I hadn't. They worked, flipping hypnotically back and forth. They didn't keep the windshield clean, but they did their best.

Plum sighed occasionally in her sleep, and made little purring noises. She shifted in her seat and wound up with her head against my shoulder, her little body curled up beside me. In sleep her face looked even younger and more completely innocent than it did when she was awake. I put a paternal arm around her. I thought of Minna, I thought of Kitty. I removed the arm and kept both hands on the wheel.

I went on driving. The rain stopped again, and shortly thereafter the sky lightened up and dawn broke rather abruptly. I thought about food. At first I just sort of thought about it, as one will, and then it began to become an obsession. I thought about the last meal I had eaten, and calculated the number of hours that had elapsed since then, and remembered the ingredients of that last meal, and compared it with other meals, and began to consider all of the meals I had eaten over the course of my life, and remembered what one after another of them had tasted like, the appearance and aroma of the various foods. I thought of the cheese and the ham sandwich which I had abandoned in the coffin. I cursed myself for abandoning them. I devised plans for returning to the grave and digging them up again. I was not wholly irrational—I *knew* that this was absurd, but I was driving on a dull road with nothing to do but think, and my body was determined that those thoughts would concern food, since that was what it wanted, and there didn't seem to be anything I could do about it.

I knew very well that this was foolish. The human body can easily go a month without food. I have occasionally fasted for three or four days at a time for one reason or another, and while there are things I would rather do, it's painless and harmless. You just need the right mental attitude, that's all. And that was the one thing I didn't have now. The human body can go a month without food, but the human mind isn't that reasonable.

I looked at Plum and wondered if she was as hungry as I was. She was asleep, and thus didn't know if she was hungry or not. I wished her name didn't happen to be the name of a sort of food. I looked at her shoulder. It was the color of a toasted English muffin. I found myself wondering what human flesh tasted like.

Plum went right on sleeping. The sun came up and blazed through her window without waking her. She didn't wake up until we ran out of gas.

This was somewhat less surprising than it may sound. It will happen to any car if you drive it long enough without filling the tank, and on a road totally lacking in filling stations it's just a question of time. Or miles, more precisely. The VW was a recent enough model to possess a gas gauge, and for the past couple of hours I had watched the needle hover closer and closer to the big E. Eventually it touched the E with no discernible decline in performance, and I had just about decided that the blessed bug would run without gas when it coughed dryly, uttered a droll belch, and quit on me. I popped it into neutral and managed to coast to the crest of a slight rise, passed the crest, and rolled on for about a half mile. It did this rather well, but it finally stopped, as everything does, and Plum woke up and asked where we were and why we had stopped. I told her, and she said that was nice. She wasn't asleep, but she wasn't exactly awake, either.

"Almost two hundred miles," I said. "That's not bad at all, really."

"Perhaps we can stop another car and get more petrol."

"There aren't any other cars. I haven't seen another car in a hundred miles." I cleared my throat. "I don't understand it, actually. The road is flat and wide and perfectly paved, and it doesn't look as though there's ever been another car on it."

"Perhaps we are the first."

"It certainly looks that way."

"You see, the road does not go anywhere, Evan."

"Huh?"

"The Retriever built it. Knanda Ndoro. Your country and many others gave him much money, and he built things throughout the nation for the glory of Modonoland."

"I thought he just kept the money."

"Some he spent on the country. There were beautification projects and modernization projects and improvement projects and, oh, many projects. You know the cultural museum in the square? This was built with aid from the Soviet Union."

"There's no roof on it," I said.

"There was not enough money to complete it."

"Oh."

"And this road, it was built with money from your country. It extends to the Congo border. But there is nothing there, you see. Just jungle. It was hoped that the government of the Congo would build a road to join up with it, but they replied that no one really wished to drive from the Congo to Modonoland anyway, or from Modonoland to the Congo, and so the road simply goes to the border and stops."

"Just like that."

"Yes."

"It must have cost millions."

"I think it did."

"And the U.S. gave you the money?"

"Yes. Knanda Ndoro announced that if he did not get the funds from you, then he would accept them from Communist China."

"Oh, well," I said. "We had no choice, did we?"

We left the car and set out along the road. It was concrete, but it should have been yellow brick. I felt like one of Dorothy's chums en route to the Emerald City. The Cowardly Lion, I decided, because the others never got hungry.

A ways down the road we saw a few columns of smoke off to the left. We found a path cutting off in that direction and took it. The terrain was rather attractive, with high savanna grasses interrupted by an occasional squat palm tree. The grass was shoulder high on me and came to the top of Plum's head.

The path led to a clearing where a scattering of geometrically precise huts circled a common cooking fire. Women squatted on their haunches around the fire baking bread. There didn't seem to be any men around.

"You know the language," I said to Plum. "See what you can do."

The hell she knew the language. It turned out that she knew English and Swahili and Modono. So did I. So didn't the women; they spoke a pleasant-sounding singsong dialect without a single recognizable word in it. Plum looked at me and shrugged.

"You will be a help to me," I said, "because you know the language."

Plum examined the ground at her feet. I smiled at the women and made eating motions. They smiled back at me and repeated the motions. I rubbed my stomach, put my fingers to my mouth, and panted like a dog. They giggled. Plum kept studying the earth.

They brought us bread baked from flour made from some sort of roots. It was bland and very dry, but tasted as though it probably had a comfortingly high protein content. Another woman brought a jug of blood-colored liquid, bubbling with fermentation and with a faint aftertaste of carrion. If the bread hadn't been quite so dry I might have passed on this, but it was impossible to get it down without liquid, so I took an optimistically hearty drink. The first gulp was a trial, but it got better as you went along.

We were still eating when the men came back. They had been hunting but didn't seem to have caught anything. The woman who seemed to be in charge explained our presence to several of the men, and they came and grunted, and I smiled and grunted back at them, and I drew a map in the dirt to show where we had come from, and they filled in details on the map. I put a mark where I had left the car and managed to convey to them what the car was and where I had left it and that they might find something of use there. I figured they could find it as worthwhile to strip an abandoned car as the kids do in my neighborhood, but I'm not sure whether or not they got the point. They didn't seem all that excited about it.

They gave us a couple of hunks of bread to take with us. A tiny boy, naked and giggling, presented Plum with a small lizard and raced back to his hut. We couldn't decide what we were supposed to do with the lizard. The only things we could think of were to eat him, make a pet of him, or pray to him. None appealed, so when we were well on our way we let him go, and he disappeared immediately in the tall grasses.

Plum said, "They were very nice. I wish we had had something to give them in return. I was afraid they might, oh, kill us or something."

"They were friendly."

"How could you tell?"

"When they befriended us and gave us food, I knew. Just like that."

"I mean before, silly."

"Who knew?"

We angled back toward the road but never quite got there. We stayed with the path we were on. It was a perfect day, with a high hot sun and a breeze that rippled the grass around us. We saw small herds of animals grazing, antelopes of one sort or another. Now and then a hawk would circle overhead. It was calm and clear and absolutely silent.

Just before nightfall we saw buzzards gathering ahead of us on the right. We approached quietly. An antelope lay in a bloody circle of trampled grass, gutted and lifeless. The lion that had made the kill was somewhere sleeping it off now, and a pair of hyenas were worrying what it had left behind. The hyenas looked formidable, but I ran at them, bellowing like a bull, and they turned tail and ran. I cut some steaks from the antelope's haunches and wiped the blade of the Swiss Army pocketknife on the beast's hide. Plum looked at the meat in my hand and made a face.

"Steak," I said happily. "I wish we had a knapsack or something. There's meat enough to last for weeks if we could only take it along."

"I hope you don't expect me to eat that, Evan."

"Of course."

"It's dead meat."

"A few hours dead."

"From an animal in the jungle. A wild animal."

I took her chin in my fingers and looked at her. "Plum," I said, "all meat comes from dead animals."

"When you buy it in the store, you don't have to think about it."

"Plum, this is your country, for Christ's sake."

"I know."

"I mean—"

"I know," she said.

When it began turning dark we picked a spot for the night. We camped near a scraggly wali tree, and I used dead leaves and twigs to get a fire started. Once it was blazing nicely I began ripping off parts of the tree and feeding them to the fire. We shishkebabed the antelope meat and Plum overcame any objections she may have had to it. I pulled up grass and cut palm fronds and made a bed for her beside the fire. She lay down on it and looked expectantly at me. I sat next to the fire and fed it with a couple of handfuls of dry grass.

"Are you coming to sleep?"

I said I would sit up awhile.

"I want you to sleep with me, Evan."

"I am not tired."

"That is not what I mean."

I looked at her. "Oh," I said, light dawning. "Plum, don't be silly."

"You do not like me."

"Of course I like you."

"You do not think I am pretty?"

"You're very pretty."

"You do not care for my body."

"Plum, you're just a kid. You're fifteen years old, for heaven's sake." I had this very strange and quite uncomfortable feeling in my throat, and the beginning of a headache. "You go to sleep now," I said. "I'll tend the fire."

"I cannot sleep," she said. And I thought she was going to say something else, but she didn't, and when I looked at her again she was out. She lay on her back, her hands clenched into little fists at her sides, and she slept.

Chapter 5

At one village the head man wore polished wooden hoop earrings and spoke a sort of pidgin Dutch. "I know Sheena," he said. "A moon is born and dies, and another, and another, and another, and another." He drew five moons in the dirt with a sharpened stick. "Sheena comes from the place of trees and vines. She kills with the sun and rides off with the moon. I am told she roasts babies and eats their flesh, and hacks off the breasts of the women, and the private parts of men. I am also told what she does with them, but I see none of this with my own eyes, and do not believe or disbelieve. For men's words are carried upon the wind, and some wind is always blowing, is it not so?"

And at another village where the women were ornamented with ridges of clay beneath the skin and where no one spoke anything which I could understand, the name *Sheena* brought a volley of gasps, an embarrassed silence, and, finally, a brusque gesture, a pointing toward the northwest.

So the white goddess, the Queen of the Jungle, seemed more than a figment of the Chief's imagination. The general consensus seemed to be that she and her gang were somewhere to the northwest, somewhere beyond the plain where the tropical rain forest began. I would have liked to ask about Sam Bowman and Knanda Ndoro, but even without a language barrier that would have been hard to manage. *"Did two black men pass through here? Or one black man?"* Wonderful.

In a way, we seemed to be on the right track. But only in a way. Imagine, if you will, that we were supposed to search in a coal mine for a black cat that wasn't there. Well, we were heading for the coal mine. Progress of a sort, but nothing to get excited about.

I didn't particularly mind, because there were other things to get excited about. Mornings, for instance, with the sun suddenly breaking above the eastern horizon, and the sure songs of birds in the thickets, early birds in swift pursuit of late worms. Animal sounds in the brush, and drums pulsing in the distance, and rainstorms that blew up suddenly just before sunset, lashing the earth for twenty or forty minutes, then ending as abruptly as they had begun.

Meals of sweet overripe melons, mahogany on the outside, salmon pink within. Plump water birds that bobbed in a muddy stream and held the pose trustingly while one shied a stone at them. Roasted over a wood fire they tasted rather like duck, which I suppose they were.

The warmth, the space, the silence. There were lions about, and hostile tribes, and things that went bump in the night, and yet from the onset I felt completely at ease in that open country. It was unpeopled and unpaved, and it let me remember that I was alive. If we never found Sheena, if the jungle had swallowed Sam Bowman, if the Retriever was lost and his treasure irretrievable, that was fine. And if I never got back to civilization, that wasn't so bad either.

The weather had something to do with this. And the good food, and the open spaces, and the friendship of the natives we met. Each gave rise to a very real pleasure. But let's be honest, huh? None of these pleasures quite compared to that of lying naked in the tall grass with Miss Pelham Jenkins and making, uh, love.

Look, it wasn't my idea.

It really wasn't, and left to my own devices I don't think it would have happened. I am not saying it never would have occurred to me. All manner of things occur to a person, whether or not he has any intentions of doing anything about them. And Plum was a particularly lovely thing, and I had noticed this. It had come to mind that Plum would one day make someone or other very happy in some bed or other, but my own appreciation of this fact was quite impersonal. She was this kid who had helped me get out of a coffin and who was now keeping me company on a Cook's Tour of Modonoland. But mainly she was a kid.

Right?

I thought so, but she wouldn't buy it.

"You think I am a child," she said, that first morning in the wild. "But I am fifteen years old. I am going to be sixteen years old."

"God willing."

"Pardon?"

"Everybody who is fifteen years old is well on the way to being sixteen," I said. "It's the natural order of things."

"You are mocking me, Evan."

"Not exactly."

"Perhaps in your country a girl my age would be a child, but in Modonoland I am a woman. Girls younger than I are married."

"But not to me."

"Have you never made love to a girl of fifteen?"

"Yes."

"You have? Then it is me you despise, and you pretend it is my age, and—"

"Twenty years ago, I slept with a girl who was fifteen."

"Oh."

"But not since then, Plum."

"Perhaps you will be able to remember how it is done, Evan."

And another time—

"Evan? I have been thinking about this matter between us. I do not think you have been honest with me at all."

"Oh?"

"I think you have been saying one thing and meaning another."

"What do you mean, Plum?"

"It is certainly a common attitude here. It is universal in Modonoland. And I understand that the situation is very much the same in America. But I thought you were different, Evan, and it saddens me to find out that you are not."

"What are you talking about?"

"That you do not want to make love to me because of my color," she said. "That is obvious. You pretend that it is my age, but I cannot believe that. You say it to spare me pain. That is all."

"Plum, that's ridiculous."

"It is a problem I will always face in this country. Black men wish to have nothing to do with a girl who is partly white. White men wish to have nothing to do with a girl who is partly black. Perhaps in another country I will find a place for myself. Or perhaps I will find a man who does not let color bother him."

"Damn it, Plum—"

"Please do not talk of it, Evan. Not now. Do you see that tree? I wonder if the fruit can be eaten."

And another time, late at night:

"Evan?"

"Can't you sleep, Plum?"

"I am all tense. My muscles are in knots."

"Try to relax."

"I cannot. It is sexual tension, you understand."

"Oh, are we back on that topic again?"

"When a woman is accustomed to sex, it is a hardship to do without it. You must know this. And have I not told you that I ceased long ago to be a virgin?"

"You told me."

"Which makes your scruples so foolish, but I will

not discuss that now. But I am so tense. If you could give me a massage to relax me . . ."

I squatted next to her and rubbed her little back. Her skin was warm velvet. I rubbed her back and found that I was grinding my teeth. I stopped grinding my teeth.

"I took off all my clothes," she said. "I hope you do not mind."

"It doesn't matter to me," I said.

"So I thought. Since I do not exist for you as a sex object, you are untouched by my nudity. So I thought."

"Well, you were right."

"Yes. I enjoy the feeling of your hands on me."

"I'm glad."

"It is very pleasant," she said. She rolled over suddenly and my hands were on her breasts. "Oh, Evan," she said. "Oh, Evan, I love you."

Her mouth was warm and urgent and greedy. Her fingers hurried with buttons and zipper. I slipped out of my clothes and lay down beside her. My hands returned to her breasts. She thrust her hips forward, urged the warmth of her loins against me. A lot of little voices inside my head started talking at once, arguing with one another. The loudest of them all said, *"Look, dummy, this is certainly a dumb time to start being a saint."*

I kissed her mouth. I kissed her throat. I kissed her little brown breasts. She made purring sounds and I kissed her and stroked her. Her legs opened and her thighs beat at me like moths at a lighted window. Another little voice, a last little voice, asked me petulantly what I thought I was getting into, and what I was getting into was Plum, and it was very nice, very nice indeed.

Afterward I put some more sticks on the fire and we shared the melon we had put aside for breakfast. Her flesh glowed pornographically in the firelight. She bit into the melon and the juice trickled down her face and onto her body.

She looked marvelous.

"Well," she said, between mouthfuls. "That wasn't so bad at all, was it?"

"You lied."

"Did I?"

"A woman of the world. A woman who ceased long ago to be a virgin."

"It seems long ago," she said, thoughtfully.

"It seems like twenty minutes or so."

"Perhaps."

"A woman strangled by sexual frustration. *'When a woman is accustomed to sex, it is a hardship to do without it.'* Teller of untruths."

"It was a pre-truth." She giggled suddenly and melon juice cascaded onto her breasts. "You would not have done it otherwise, would you?"

"I don't know."

I reached for her. She squirmed loose, giggling. I caught her and she threw her arms around my neck. Melon juice got all over us, but we didn't notice this until quite a while later.

When she said, "You wouldn't have done it if you

knew. Or not right away, it would have taken more provocation, and it was hard enough to provoke you as it was. And I wanted us to do this. It is silly not to, don't you think? We are all alone in the middle of the country and we should be close together, and are we not close now?"

"We are," I agreed.

"And you love me, don't you, Evan?"

"Uh-huh."

"And it does not disturb you that I am of color?"

"Of course not."

"Or that I am fourteen?"

"Fourteen?"

She put her hand on my arm. "You are angry with me."

"I—"

"It too was a pre-truth. Fourteen going on fifteen. Everyone who is fourteen years old is well on the way to being fifteen. It is the natural order of things."

I didn't say anything. She curled up against me and her head nestled in the crook of my arm. She smelled wonderfully of damp earth and matted grass and left-over love. She said sleepily, "Fourteen, fifteen, just numbers. The number of times the sun goes around the earth."

"I think it's the other way around."

"Oh. All right. I think I will go to sleep now. I love you. Good night."

She went at once to sleep, as she was apt to do. I lay awake breathing her smell and tending the fire and listening to predators howling in the distance. I felt an unwelcome kinship to them. I told myself I was a dirty old man and that what had happened this night would not be repeated.

And I told myself the very same thing the next morning, and the next night, and so on each morning and each evening, as we screwed our way into the heart of the country.

Chapter 6

The weather was really fantastic. I had expected it to be too hot, it being summer in Africa, but from the vantage point of a New York winter I had figured that too hot was just right. It wasn't, though, not where we were. It was hot but not too hot, and it rained for about an hour a day, and the general climatic conditions were rather like Southern California.

People move to California at an extraordinary rate, while hardly anybody ever goes to Modonoland. You might think there are reasons.

There are reasons.

More reasons, in fact, than one can shake a stick at. A cloud of biting flies, for example, to cite a reason at which we actually tried shaking a stick. I don't know where the cloud of biting flies came from, or why, but in the middle of an otherwise unblemished afternoon they were suddenly upon us, doing as biting flies are wont to do. Flailing at them with our hands did no good. Beating at them with sticks did no good. Waiting for them to go away seemed overly passive.

Plum said, "Run!"

"It's no use. They can move faster than we can. They—"

"Run!"

She ran off to her left at full speed, wagging her hands at the flies as she did so. I ran after her. The flies, like the poor, were always with us.

"This way!"

She darted. I followed. There were some trees, and there was a gap in the trees, and there was a still pool through the gap in the trees. Plum plunged in. I followed. The pool was about four feet deep with a soft stoneless bottom. We crouched with just our faces showing, and the flies decided to make do with our faces. When I tried slapping them away from my face, they settled on my hand.

"Get my knife, Evan. And cut those reeds. They are hollow and we can breathe through them."

I did, and they were, and we could and did. We crouched with our heads below the surface and breathed through the reeds, and I considered just how far I had come. Not too many days ago I had been in a coffin breathing through a metal tube, and now I was in a pool breathing through a hollow reed, and who could say what the future might hold.

Every once in a while I would come up to check on the flies, and for a long time they were still there, and then they weren't. Plum straightened up and we looked at each other. We were wet and filthy and covered with fly bites.

"This pool," I said.

"Filthy water."

"But it kept us from getting eaten alive, which is probably what would have happened. They did a pretty

good job on us as it was. How did you know to run for
water?"

"It seemed the thing to do."

"And how did you know that the water would be
here? You ran straight toward it. And how did you know
the reeds would be hollow?"

She straightened up, beamed. "I am African," she
said.

"So?"

"Certain knowledge is inborn, Evan." She tilted her
head. "This is my country, you see. I sense things. I am
able to react intuitively. You, a white man, would not
understand."

I nodded at this. Plum started for the bank. I put a
hand on her wrist, tugged. She started to say something. I shhhed her, pointed in the direction she was
going, then led her carefully in the other direction to
the bank. She scrambled out and collapsed on the bank.
The crocodile she had almost bumped into went on
sunning himself.

"We are very fortunate," she said. "He was just a few
yards from us. People are often eaten by crocodiles."

"If not by flies."

"I never considered that there might be a crocodile
in the water."

"Crocodiles. There are quite a few of them, actually." I pointed some out. "All sizes," I said.

"I led us into the middle of a crocodile pool."

"Any port in a storm."

"A pool of crocodiles—" She trembled. I put a wet
arm around her. It didn't do anything to stop the trem-

bling. Then at once she straightened, narrowed her eyes.

"I am Welsh," she said. "Well brought up young Welsh ladies know nothing of crocodiles."

The flies didn't turn out to be tsetse flies. Or, if they were, they were out of condition, because neither of us got sleeping sickness. It had occurred to me that we might. I spent a while wondering idly what would happen if we did. Would my lack of a sleep center change the form of the disease, or did it work upon another organ? Either way, I thought, we would very probably die of it. The poetic implications of the death by sleeping sickness of a hard-core insomniac were by no means lost on me. I did not, though, much appreciate them.

But all the flies gave us were fly bites. Which was enough. The bites were red and itched. I was afraid they might get infected. They didn't, but they didn't get better, either. Plum put wet mud on them to take the sting out. This was one of her less successful Afro bits. It didn't work at all. We went on itching until we ran into a hunting party from one of the eastern tribes. One of their number gathered leaves from a shrub, boiled them, let the solution cool, and put it on our bites. They stopped itching immediately and healed completely in a matter of hours. It was damned impressive, really.

It was, I guess, two days after the treatment of the fly bites that Plum fell in the lion pit. There was really no way to avoid it. Whoever dug the thing concealed it perfectly, and Plum and I were walking along a path, and I was making little grabs at her body, and she was giggling happily and darting on ahead, and abruptly the earth opened up under her feet and she disappeared. I dashed forward and looked down, and the sight was reassuringly anticlimactic. The pit had been furnished with sharpened stakes, but they were literally few and far between, and Plum had fallen between a batch of them. And it wasn't too deep, and she had landed without breaking anything, so she was all right. But she wasn't happy.

I got her out and dusted her off and we pressed onward, a little less enthusiastically than before. It seemed that every day we were pressing on with a little less enthusiasm.

That night she lay in my arms and sighed. I told her she seemed a little weary.

"Sure I get weary," she said, "wearing the same old dress. Really, Evan, I am beginning to despise my clothing. It is falling apart. And yours too, I think."

"Yes."

"I think it was a bad idea washing them in that stream. Next time we wash them it would be good to determine first if the water is clean, and if it has an odor."

"Next time we'll take a helicopter."

She didn't say anything. We lay there together in silence. Mosquitoes buzzed us and we waved them away. Earlier on, a wizened gap-toothed man had explained that we might keep mosquitoes away by putting carrion in the fire. They weren't supposed to like this, for which I could scarcely blame them. The idea was that you carried around a little sack of spoiled flesh, and at night you kept throwing chunks of it into the fire. The mosquitoes would have had to be a lot worse before we tried this.

Plum did look weary. I dismissed feelings of lechery and turned on paternalism and gave her a passionless hug. "We should be at the mission soon," I said.

"And then?"

"Well, they'll feed us. And it ought to be possible to get a bath and some fresh clothes."

"And the latest word on Sheena."

"That too."

She looked up at me. Ever since the high grasses had begun giving way to jungle, her spirits had gradually dampened along with the terrain. No doubt the flies had had something to do with it, and the lion pit, and the unfortunate stream where we had washed our clothes.

She said, "Do you believe there is a Sheena?"

"Yes. Too many different tribesmen have described her. Too many people have reacted to her name."

"Legends spread widely in this country, Evan."

"I think there's a girl to go with this one. Of course you have to expect a certain amount of distortion. The stories these people tell—after all, the tribes in this area are on the primitive side, and the white goddess bit lends itself to exaggeration. I wouldn't be surprised if Sheena is your color or darker, with, say, prematurely gray hair. And if her whole movement, instead of being the wild terrorist gang we've heard described, isn't just a new cult-religion."

"But everyone has been so terrified."

"Well, remember the watchamacallit? The Nishanti? The clowns beating bones on the ground in the cemetery?"

"Yes?"

"Well, imagine how terrifying a cult like that could be by the time the story got to be fifth or sixth hand. Or take it from another angle, imagine the story they're telling about the corpse that walked out of its grave. Nothing like that has happened in almost two thousand years, and—"

"Evan?"

"What?"

"Shall we find your friends?"

"They're not exactly my friends. I never met either of them before."

"Then how will you know them?"

"They're both tall," I said. "And black."

She looked at me.

"Hell," I said. "I think we can assume that any two tall black men out here who speak English are odds-on to be Knanda Ndoro and Sam Bowman. And I've got a recognition signal to bounce off Bowman. He doesn't know I exist, but when I give him the password he'll know that he is to trust me."

"A password. It sounds—"

"It sounds kind of Mickey Mouse," I suggested.

"I do not understand."

"It sounds cornball. Silly and, uh, oh, like something out of a crumby movie."

"Mickey Mouse," she said.

"Right."

"I know that mouse from the movies. He can speak,

but his dog cannot speak. I have never understood that."

"Well, it's too subtle for an African girl."

Her hand moved quickly. "If I were Sheena," she said, mock-savagely, "I would cut this off."

"Don't even talk like that."

"But I am not Sheena," she said, "and must think of something better to do. Help me think of something, Evan. Oh, Evan—"

Two nights later, as the sun was just dropping out of sight in the west, we came into view of the mission. We reached the top of a small rise and looked down across a few hundred yards of cleared fields to a trio of squat concrete-block buildings. The Père Julien Mission, staffed with Belgian priests and nuns and nurses. I planted my feet and looked across at the mission and felt like Balboa, silent upon a peak in Darien. Like Brigham Young, catching his first glimpse of Utah. Like Moses upon Mount Nebo. I searched for words appropriate to the occasion.

"That's the place," I said.

"Is that all?"

"What did you expect? Loew's 83rd?"

"Pardon?"

"What I mean is that this isn't so bad for the middle of the jungle. Three buildings, and they're of pretty good size, and some plowed fields with things growing in them, and I suppose they've got some animals, probably chickens in that shed over on the left and maybe some goats or cows. After all, it's been a while since we've seen anything you could call a building. Or anything you could call a meal, as far as that goes. I know it isn't much when you're used to a metropolis like Griggstown, but—"

"You are making fun of me."

"A little bit."

"But I did think it would be more, oh, I don't know."

I knew what she meant. We had been building the mission up in our minds to the point where it loomed as the end of the journey. In the course of the past two days we had run into perhaps a half dozen groups of natives, none of whom we could quite communicate with but all of whom kept pointing us toward the mission. We also managed to gather, between the grunts and ersatz-pidgin phrases, that (a) Sheena was in the area, (b) they would know of this in the mission, and (c) something very exciting was going to happen. So if they had scored the whole thing for a movie, there would have been this gradual drum roll picking up in volume and tempo until we reached that peak, and then the music would stop and the camera would move for a long shot of the mission, and there would be these three dumpy little blockhouses.

The closer we got to the mission, the more it reminded me of a movie set. I couldn't avoid the feeling that these three buildings were false fronts with nothing behind them. The place was obviously not abandoned—a heap of weeds drying in the dying sun could not have been pulled more than a few hours ago. And yet there was a feeling of utter desolation.

"I'm afraid," Plum said in a still small voice, changing once again from woman to child. And put her hand in mine, and held on tight.

I called out, "Hello!" I called out similar words and phrases in French and in Flemish.

There was no answer.

"Evan, perhaps they are at their prayers."

"Perhaps."

I started forward. Plum's hand stopped me. "It would not do to interrupt them, Evan."

"Well, I'll just see what—"

"Perhaps we should wait until morning."

"What's the matter with you?"

Her face was drawn, her lip trembling. "I don't know. I don't think we should go in there."

"Why not?"

"I told you I don't know."

"That's ridiculous," I said. I called out again in Flemish. I uncurled Plum's fingers and took my hand back. I trotted on to the doorway of the nearest and smallest building, calling things out as I went.

There was a buzzing sound, the droning of flies. The door was ajar. I gave it a gentle shove and it swung open. The buzzing got louder. I looked down and saw the flies swarming around the girl's leg.

The rest of the girl was a few yards away on the right. And past her, scattered here and there around the room, were the others.

Chapter 7

*P*lum screamed for about three quarters of an hour, pausing intermittently to vomit. She would throw back her head and shriek and wail, eyes rolling, nails digging into palms, tears streaming down face, and then the screams would break abruptly off and she would toss her head forward like a robin bobbin' along, and then she would throw up. Followed by more screaming.

I couldn't blame her. I spent a while trying to calm her down, and when that proved impossible I made her as comfortable as she was likely to get while I took a look around the place and surveyed the damage, which was total. When I took a head count, and I wish I did not mean that as literally as I do, I came up with a tally of thirty-four dead, twenty-five women and nine men.

They were not merely dead. Death in itself is chilling to look upon, however inoffensive and antiseptic the form it takes. But these men and women had been torn apart. It was not always possible to tell what belonged to whom.

I had seen this sort of thing before. In war movies soldiers die neatly of invisible wounds, but when I was in Korea death was apt to be messy. I can still remember the sight of a group of fellows who had been playing cards when a shell landed among the four of them. The task of sorting and compiling their bodies for shipment home was largely arbitrary. Like the Belgian priests and nuns and nurses, they had been made a hash of.

Yet this was different. A shell, a bomb, an explosive charge—these are essentially impersonal affairs, and if they make death a messy business they do so with no special malice.

Sheena had acted with malice. The carnage in the three buildings was the work not of a single explosive charge but of uncountable blows with knife and ax and machete, so that each aspect of the outrage had a very personal stamp upon it. All of the bodies had been decapitated, and most arms and legs had been hacked off as well. The women had been separated from their breasts. In similar fashion, the men had been emasculated, but in their case the organs of which they had been deprived were nowhere to be found. Sheena seemed to have taken them along, for reasons I did not care to consider.

I didn't get sick. I felt the way I do when I drink too much strong coffee, all tightly strung and jittery. I paced from one building to another, stopping to comfort Plum, then moving on again, and I looked at flesh and blood over and over again until it lost its impact. Then I found Plum and took hold of her. She was still hysterical. I held her chin in one hand and slapped her face with the other. She clutched me and gasped and stopped the sobbing and caught hold of herself.

"Come on," I said. "Let's go."

"Where?"

"Let's just get the hell out of here, that's all. Back the way we came, I suppose."

"But—"

"At least we know the route. We'll try not to fall in the lion pit or get eaten by the flies. I don't know how long it'll take, but the sooner we get going, the sooner we'll be there."

"Where? Griggstown?"

"For a starter."

"But we will be arrested there."

"Not if we don't announce ourselves. We'll get out of the country, don't worry. You can go to London or come to America or whatever you want."

"But what about your friends, Evan?"

"My friends?"

"Sam Bowman and Knanda Ndoro."

I started to tell her that they weren't my friends, then gave it up as irrelevant. "They're dead," I said.

"You have found their bodies?"

I shook my head. "But I don't give them much chance. The stories they tell about this Sheena are pure understatement. You saw what her gang did here." She began to go green again, so I hurried on. "If Bowman and the Retriever met up with the White Goddess you could bury what's left of them in a matchbox." The image did little for Plum's complexion. "And if they didn't run up against Sheena, then we've got even less chance of finding them. It would be a case of not knowing which haystack to look in for the needle. I would say that either they're out of the country, in which case we can forget about finding them, or Sheena got them, in which case they've joined their ancestors. But in either case—"

"We should leave this place."

"You're on the right track now."

She nodded. I thought she was nodding in agreement, and then I saw that her eyes had gone glassy, and she nodded again and started to pitch forward on her face. I caught her. She swayed dizzily and sagged against me. I held onto her.

She said, "I'm all right now."

"Uh-huh."

"Evan, I cannot go anywhere now. And we do not dare to travel by night. We are not that fine at getting around in jungles to begin with, is it not so? And by night it would be much worse." She took a breath. "We shall begin our journey in the morning."

"I think we should go now."

She raised her eyes beseechingly. "I do not think I could do this, Evan. I am so tired."

"But if they—"

"I must sleep, Evan." She blinked rapidly. "We both must sleep. I am sure that you too are exhausted, although it is possible you do not realize it."

"Oh, I realize it."

"For you are under strain and may be living on your nerves, Evan, but I know that you need a night's sleep. You have slept so little since we left Griggstown. Whenever I look at you you are wide awake. I do not think that I have ever seen you sleeping."

"Oh, I hibernate."

"What is that?"

"What bears do."

"Bears? Oh, yes, I know them. They live in Jellystone Park and are friends with squirrels and rangers. I have seen them in the cinema with Mickey the Mouse. They, too, can speak, can they not?"

"Uh."

"But I do not understand what it is to hibernate."

I explained what it was to hibernate, and that I was joking. I told Plum that I could get by without very much sleep, and we left it at that. My exact condition isn't precisely a state secret, but it's something I don't bring up if I can avoid it. The revelation of my insomnia always leads into a predictable pattern of questions and answers, one I've had rather enough of over the years. It is simpler to avoid all that.

Still, Plum insisted, I must need some sleep now. We could not possibly travel all night, nor would it be safe. I didn't really want to agree with this but I couldn't avoid it. She was obviously shot, and while I might have been willing to try plodding through the jungle at night on my own, I couldn't manage it with Plum slung over my shoulder.

But I didn't like the alternative a hell of a lot. The idea of spending the night in the midst of all that carnage was profoundly unappealing, and the idea of spending any unnecessary time in Sheena's neighborhood was positively chilling.

The smallest of the three buildings, a combination of chapel and office, was less gory than the other two. I parked Plum outside and did what I could to clear the building of the evidence of the massacre. Yoga has certain techniques for cultivating detachment during the performance of unpleasant tasks. I tried them, and while I couldn't entirely blind myself to what I was doing, I did manage to get through it.

I found a straw tick and some bed linen from one of the other buildings and fixed up a bed for Plum. I fetched her. She had swung all the way from hysterical to numb, and I had to pick her up and carry her to the chapel and tuck her into her bed. She lay down, then propped herself up on one elbow and scanned the room.

"All gone," she said.

"What is?"

"The dead bodies. Gone. Good."

She flopped down and closed her eyes. I sat beside her for a few minutes. Then I got to my feet and walked quietly out of there.

It was growing dark now, the sky darkening rather abruptly as is its wont in that region. I went to the garden to pull some vegetables but stopped myself when I realized that I wasn't really hungry. We hadn't eaten anything substantial in quite a while, but somehow the thought of food was in and of itself enough to appease the desire for food. I examined the turnipish root I had pulled and decided that nothing could induce me to eat it. I dropped it and went into the middle building.

I guess it must have been the infirmary. It was hard to say for certain; all three buildings had evidently played mutiple roles, and everything was presently a complete mess. I tried to ignore the corpses and began searching the place without any conscious objective in mind. I was looking for something but it didn't much matter what it was. The Holy Grail, the Golden Fleece, the Fountain of Youth—any of these would have done.

What I found was a combination of the three. It was a half-gallon jug of pure grain alcohol, medicinal grade, distilled in Johannesburg and certified fit for human consumption. Grain alcohol. Around two hundred proof. Bottled and capped and labeled and, in the midst of the most extraordinary display of destructive power since Nagasaki, remarkably not to say miraculously unbroken.

And I held it in my hand and looked at it, and all at once I knew what it was I had been looking for, and that this was it. The Elixir of Life. The Universal Solvent. The Final Solution.

I found a gallon of bottled spring water and a plastic coffee cup, and I took the two jugs and the cup and went back to where Plum was sleeping. She was tossing restlessly, and I put a hand on her forehead and gentled her into a more restful sleep. Then I filled the coffee cup halfway with alcohol, topped it off with spring water, and drank the result.

It tasted like vodka, which was only right, since that is what it really was. Hundred proof vodka. It burned. It had a hell of a kick to it.

I liked it.

I emptied the cup and filled it up again, this time with a touch less alcohol and a touch more water. I worked on the drink and let my mind unwind and work the knots out of itself. Just what the missionary ordered, I decided, sipping appreciatively.

I closed my eyes. The missionaries, priests and nuns alike, were now either in Heaven or not, depending upon the validity of their basic assumptions, which they were now unfortunately in a position to confirm or deny. Bowman, my more or less fellow agent, was probably dead. So was Knanda Ndoro, the Retriever of Modonoland.

As the alcohol assumed its rightful place in my bloodstream, it became clear to me that I did not very much care about Sam Bowman—if he was a real secret agent, death was part of the game, and if he was a fraud, *sic semper bolonis*. Nor did I care if Knanda Ndoro got his, or if his royal treasury was lost forever. Royal treasuries are fun, but this one looked to be more trouble than it was worth, and farther out of reach than any grapes to any fox, as far as that went.

Nor, finally, did I really care about the missionaries. The only bothersome thing about Sheena's annihilation of them was that Plum and I had walked in on its aftermath. Had I been in New York at the time, they could have died in the news without upsetting me a whole hell of a lot. A missionary, after all, assumes much the same sort of an occupational risk as does a secret agent or an African dictator. There is always the possibility that martyrdom will pave the road to sainthood, anyway.

I filled the cup and looked at it like Hamlet at Yorick. I sipped, and shuddered at the stuff, which I had perhaps not diluted as much as I'd intended, and swallowed, and shuddered again, and then basked in the flow of warmth from my middle. The alcohol brought an awful clarity of vision. I was in Modonoland, I realized now, for no good purpose whatsoever. The whole venture was stupidly negative. I had come here because I had not liked where I was, and because everything had been getting worse, and because I wanted to go someplace warm. I had fled from the implication that I might have ambivalent feelings toward my ersatz daughter, Minna, and had retaliated by taking a fourteen-year-old mistress. I had—

I had gone off, I saw now, on a particularly witless tangent.

And it was time to get back on the main road.

My mind worked as quickly as it could, stumbling now and again but plunging on undaunted. First things, I decided, first. I would begin setting my house in order and making some sort of logical pattern for my life. I would get out of the jungle and back to civilization, and I would find a place for Plum, and I would return to New York and marry Kitty and adopt Minna and move out of the mad jungle that was Manhattan. I could picture myself in some clean and neat suburban community in Jersey or Connecticut, say. A comfortable little ranch house. Steaks grilling over charcoal in the backyard. A power mower shaving the grass in front. Children gamboling like lambs over the back lawn.

I drank again and thought of Peter Pan. If you grew up you couldn't fly. Well, it was time I grew up, and maybe it was time I stopped flying. A house in the suburbs, a wife, a family, a station wagon, a snow blower, a freezer, a power hedge trimmer, a dishwasher, a family room, a color television set, a breakfast nook—I closed my eyes and saw all the trappings of the good life fitting themselves into the picture, explaining and defining me. No more a ratty apartment on West 107th Street. No more crazy-quilt political organizations. No more chaos, no more anarchy.

No more trips to places like this one.

After a while I capped both jugs and slipped out of the building without waking Plum. There was no moon in view, but the sky was bright with stars. I was just beginning to get used to the southern skies, just beginning to recognize the various constellations. I looked up at them now and imagined myself in my spacious tree-shaded back yard in, say, Paramus, gazing up at the stars and contemplating the merits of pre-emergence crabgrass killer.

It sounds, I suppose, like a joke, but it was a joke I had given off laughing over long ago, and old jokes tend to become new truths. I had always wondered why sooner or later everyone packed it in and went to the suburbs. Everyone did this because sooner or later everyone realized that it was the only sensible thing to do. Sooner or later everyone realized that one had to put points on one's compass and chart the course of one's life. If it had taken me rather more time than usual, well, that might even be all to the good; it would give me things to look back fondly on in old age.

My head buzzed with plans. Cancel the League for the Restoration of Cilician Armenia; substitute the Parent-Teacher Association. Cross out the Internal Macedonian Revolutionary Organization and write in the Flat Hills Country Club. I could see it all now, and it all looked good. Charge accounts, color-coordinated bathrooms, labor-saving devices—all the little human touches that separate us from the apes.

If any doubts attempted to surface, I was too involved with my vision to pay them mind. I went back for the alcohol, cut it with some water, drank. I drifted outside again and wandered beneath the stars, only to return again for another drink. After quite a long while of this, the birds began singing their heads off. It was still perfectly dark when they did this, but I guess they knew something, because after about fifteen minutes of tweet-tweet-tweet the sky turned light with dawn.

Shortly after this happened, Plum woke up with a start. That's not one of my all-time favorite expressions, but it's what she did. Heretofore she had always awakened rather gently and comfortably, I'd usually been on hand when she woke up, and of late I'd often taken an active part in waking her, in which case the mornings started out very pleasantly for both of us.

(And this, I told myself now, would have to stop. In a sense, it constituted anticipatory infidelity to Kitty, my bride and helpmate to be. Furthermore, it struck me that the recurring carnal knowledge of a fourteen-year-old Welsh-African hybrid did not quite jibe with my new role as suburban pillar.)

This morning, as I said, she woke with a start. There was this sudden thrashing about, accompanied by a volley of small yelps. I held onto her and said things like, "Easy, easy," and "It's all right," and the yelps and thrashing eased off and stopped.

"It was a dream," she said, blinking. "Everyone was being cut into bits and raped and killed and—"

"It was a dream."

She put her hand between her little breasts. "How it pounds! I cannot catch my breath."

"Are you all right?"

"I think so. What is that, Evan?"

She was pointing to my cup. "Oh," I said. "Well, it's vodka."

"Vodka? In a mission?"

I explained that I had made it out of alcohol and water, a process at least as praiseworthy in her eyes as the transmutation of water to wine. She asked if she could have some, and I told her she couldn't.

"But why?"

"You're too young," I said.

"I am old enough to be slept with but too young to have a drink?"

I considered this carefully. "You're too young to sleep with, too," I said. I spoke carefully, too, because my tongue seemed thicker than usual. "But, you see, it's a case of the smaller boll weevil."

"The smaller—"

"The lesser of two weevils," I said triumphantly.

"Evan?"

"Hmmm?"

"What is the matter with you?"

"I'm a pillar of the community."

"Are you drunk?"

"I suppose I am."

"You're talking so funny."

"Er."

She reached for the cup. I drew it away from her. A pillar of the community would not serve alcoholic beverages to minors, I told myself.

She said, "Have you been drinking all night? And you did not get to sleep at all, did you?"

"Well, I had a few hours sleep—"

"Oh, Evan, you must be tired!"

I poured out the cup of vodka, capped the two jugs, got to my feet. This last process was by far the most difficult of the three but I managed it, swaying rhythmically to and fro. I wasn't all that drunk, I decided. I was somewhere in that good gray area of insobriety, neither as sober as a judge nor as drunk as a lord. A full meal and a chance to walk off some of the alcohol would clear away the cobwebs.

"Evan, we ought to go now."

"Breakfast," I said.

"I am not hungry. The sky is light, it is morning, and I think—"

"Hungry," I said. "Eat first, then we'll talk."

"You said last night that it was dangerous to stay here."

"It is. A person could get drunk around here."

"Evan—"

"There's nothing to worry about, Plum."

"But you said—"

"Never mind what I said. What do I know?" She blinked at this. "Come on," I went on. "I'll cook us something and then we can get started."

"Where?"

"There's a kitchen in the far building."

"I do not want to go."

"Suit yourself."

"What will we eat?"

"Oh, I'll find something," I said lightly. "With all those bodies out there—"

"Evan!"

She had turned green again. I assured her that I was joking and she looked up at me, glaring balefully. I left her there and went to the kitchen, or, more precisely, the cooking area in the far building. I stepped over bodies and parts of bodies without reacting to them at all. I don't know whether this was a result of the alcohol or if I was simply becoming accustomed to their presence, as one learns not to notice the wallpaper in a rented room.

Sheena's men had found the kitchen before me, and had done what they could to kill it. The food they hadn't carried off was now decorating the walls and floors. A great many eggs and melons had been smashed almost beyond recognition. I ignored all this, whistled a happy approximation of a tune, and found a couple of eggs and a frying pan in which to scramble them. I couldn't find any salt or pepper or milk or cooking oil or, indeed, anything but the eggs, and the result was nothing James Beard would have wanted to hear about, but then he wouldn't have been too happy with anything we had eaten since leaving Griggstown. Neither, as far as that goes, were we. The eggs were better than starvation, I decided. The smaller boll weevil.

I dished them out on two presumably clean plates, scared

up a pair of forks, and went off in search of Plum. She was where I'd left her but she wasn't how I'd left her. Her eyes were glassy and she had a stupid grin on her face.

"Whee," she said. "Shmells like eggs."

"They're eggs, all right. Hey—"

She ignored the fork, took a handful of egg, stuffed it into her mouth. "Ughhh," she said.

"I'm sorry if you don't—"

"Yummy," she said. She scooped up another handful of egg and pushed it in my face. "Eat, eat," she said. "Later we'll talk."

"You've been drinking," I said.

"Jusht a little tashte."

"You've been drinking alcohol."

"I've been drinking alcohol," she agreed owlishly. "Fourteen yearsh old and I'm depraved. Drinking alcohol and running around in the jungle—"

"How much did you have?"

"—and fucking. Theshe eggsh are terrible. Are you shtill drunk?"

"I think sho. Damn it to hell. I think *so*. They aren't that bad."

"Dry and no tashte. I shouldn't have had that drink, I shupposhe. It'sh bad for both of ush to be drunk, ishn't it?"

"I guess so."

She put the plate down. "But I really feel great," she said. "Niche and looshe and everything."

"Alcohol has that effect sometimes."

"It'sh really great." She extended her arms, beaming. "I've got a really wonderful idea."

"Oh?"

"Let'sh shcrew."

"No."

"No?"

I tried explaining it to her. I don't suppose I did a very good job of it, being still half in the bag myself, but I tried to make her understand about my need for a well-ordered life, my plans to marry and settle down and acquire a power mower and a mortgage. What I said may or may not have made perfect sense, but in any case Plum couldn't make head or tail out of it, a cliché which, now that I think about it, has particular relevance under the circumstances. Her reply was nonverbal; she took off her clothes and unbuttoned my shirt and rubbed up against me.

"And besides that," I said, shifting verbal gears, "we don't have the time. It's not safe to stick around here, and we should have left a long time ago."

"You're right," she said.

"I'm glad you realize that. So—"

"We should have left lasht night, and we should have left when the shun came up this morning, and we shouldn't have shtopped to have breakfast, and you shouldn't have gotten drunk lasht night, and I shouldn't have gotten drunk this morning. But we did all thoshe things wrong, and we're shtill here, and it would be fun to make love, and I have all my clothes off, and you have most of your clothes off, and, oh, Evan, put your hand right here for a minute—"

And what I thought, since the human mind is well-equipped for letting ego figure out reasons to give id its way, was that this could serve as a line of demarcation between the old and the new. A final fling with Plum now at the apex of our adventure, and then we could head back the way we came just as I headed back to the life of the new Evan Tanner, the upright suburban Evan Tanner. One final taste of Plum Pudding and tomorrow the diet would begin.

It seemed like a good idea at the time.

"Evan?"

I sighed a long and lazy sigh and rolled over onto my side. I closed my eyes and listened to the sounds of morning—the wind in the tall grasses, the flies swarming in the other buildings.

"I think I am not drunk any longer."

"Neither am I."

"That was very nice, Evan. Does it always make one sober to make love?"

"Not always."

"We should dress now."

"We should."

"We should leave at once."

"Yes," I said. I sat up. "We really should." I reached for my clothes. "We wasted far too much time already. Not that it was exactly a waste, but we should have been out of here hours ago. Fortunately it hasn't done any—"

"Any what?"

I didn't say anything. "Evan? You stopped in the middle of a sentence."

She was facing the opposite way, her back to the doorway of the building. She couldn't see what I saw.

"Evan?"

"I was going to say harm, it hasn't done any harm. But I think it has."

"What?"

"Don't turn around," I said levelly. "Stay where you are, stay calm, don't turn around—"

So of course she turned around.

And saw what I saw:

Three men, black as power, naked as truth, and tall enough for pro basketball. Three huge naked black men with polished bones through their septa and bone rings on their fingers. Three naked black giants with their genitals painted bloody red.

Looking our way, and grinning.

Chapter 8

The thing to do, I thought, was not panic. This thought didn't do too much good. The thing to do when mountain climbing is not fall, and the thing to do when swimming is not sink, and the thing to do when menaced by three naked black giants is not panic. Sensational.

One of the giants pointed at me. "Uganda," he said, more or less. "Mobutu Kasavubu Casaba Curare Montego. Uhuru Godzilla Colorado. Antigua."

I kept my eyes on the three of them and reached blindly to my left, where I had left my pants. I fumbled in the pocket and found the Swiss Army pocketknife.

"Matilda. Piranha Daktari Laconic Malaysia Tomorrow. Llewellyn Otsego Decatur."

I opened the knife as surreptitiously as I could under the circumstances, which were not as conducive to that sort of thing as I might have wished. I got the can-opener blade first try. That wouldn't do at all. Next shot, I got the blade you use for punching holes in belts, if you've either lost some weight or stolen a fat man's belt. I decided it would do for punching holes in people as well, and that I didn't have time to search for a more conventional weapon. Besides, the belt-hole maker was certainly more useful than, say, the nail file. Or the tweezers.

I held the knife in my right hand and groped around with my left until I latched onto one of the forks with which we had been eating the lamented eggs. While all of this was going on the Modonoland Globetrotters held their ground, saying things like *Toyota* and *Kon-Tiki* and *Mechanic* to each other, and laughing their heads off between phrases. The humor was over my head, but I hoped they would stay amused. I had the feeling that the minute their sense of humor failed them they would turn ugly.

Surprise, I thought. The good old element of surprise, that's what we had going for us. They figured that we were paralyzed with fear—an understandable misconception, that—and the last thing they expected was an attack. True, there were three of them and one and a half of us. True, they were large enough to astonish a Texan. But they seemed to be unarmed, whereas I had a knife and a fork. Well, a belt punch and a fork. Well, that was something, wasn't it?

"Corona," said the one in the middle, approximately. "Melina Kandinsky Mercouri. Gowanda Kenosha Cunni—"

I attacked.

I did everything at once, because I had the feeling that there would be no second take, that all of this had to be done correctly first time around. I sprang to my feet and charged at them in one fine liquid motion, arms extended and weapons held high, face contorted in my most hideous snarl. I tore the air with a shriek designed to curdle the blood of my opponents and freeze them in their tracks. A phrase came unbidden to mind, a line from the advertisement of a factory-to-you discounter. *"It's time to cut out the middle man,"* a voice spoke inside my head, and I sprang at the middle man, fully prepared to cut him out.

The next thing I knew I had left the ground and was flying ass over teacups through the air. It was the damnedest thing ever. I never even had the sensation of physical contact with the man. Obviously he did take hold of me and throw me, but it happened so very suddenly and with such ease and precision that I was never aware of it. I even thought for a moment that I had taken flight, or that there had been an earthquake, or that the world was coming to an end. Nor was I convinced that the three possibilities were mutually exclusive. But I didn't have too much time to work things out in my head because almost immediately I hit the wall with it and crumpled up on the ground.

I got up again as quickly as I could, which wasn't very. They looked quite as they had looked before, standing in a row taking things easy, the only change being that they had turned to face me. Behind them Plum was posing as an allegorical statue representing Surprise. The man in the middle was saying things like *Salami* and *Horizon* and *Montezuma*.

So I charged again. This time I started out once again for the man in the middle; then, halfway there, like any suburbanite I drifted to the right. This, see, was strategy. I seemed to be charging blindly ahead at the man who had sent me flying, but that was just to give the man on the right a false sense of security. To lull him into inattention.

It didn't work. This time I landed on the floor instead of hitting the wall, and this time it took a few seconds longer to shake the errant confusion out of my head, and this time when I got to my feet I discovered the Swiss Army pocketknife was missing. I still had the fork, though. Otherwise everything was as before—the same extraordinary sensation of flight, the same utter rout for our side.

The man in the middle was talking again. Or maybe it was the one on the left, or the one on the right. I couldn't be sure. Nor could I catch what they were saying. Before the words had been meaningless enough, but now I couldn't even pick up on the sound. I suppose I was as close to sleep as it is possible to be while walking around, and closer than I had been in twenty years.

I looked around for my breath and couldn't quite find it, and then the one on either the right or left said something, and the one on either the left or right giggled and took a step forward, and I gathered that the third time was going to be the charm. My man thrust one foot forward and planted the other at a right angle to it. His hands assumed the traditional posture, one up in front of his face, the other just in front of his shoulder. His face, so loose and composed before, was now drawn and deeply seamed.

I did not attack this time. He was not waiting for me, either. He took small steps toward me, extending the lead foot, bringing the rear foot up, constantly maintaining the stance. I tried arranging myself similarly, wondering at the same time why I was bothering. He was going to cut me up and use me for bait and there wasn't a damned thing I could do about it.

And the hell of it was that I was never absolutely beyond redemption in hand-to-hand combat. They gave me lessons in it before they shipped me to Korea, and a couple of times on those numbered hills I had a chance to show what I had learned, and it went well enough. I was never great but I was never awful, either, but these three clowns were good enough to make my old judo instructors look like barroom brawlers.

The man came closer, and I looked at him and at the others, and I glanced among other things at his bright red genitals, and at the others' bright red genitals, and I thought again of the judo instructors and my last thought in that connection, and something clicked.

I dropped my hands. I opened my mouth and, loud and clear, I shouted out, *"Ontogeny recapitulates phylogeny!"*

Chapter 9

The three of them took the news in diverse fashion. The one approaching me with murderous intent stopped in his tracks, which was good, and blinked, which wasn't bad either. Another just stood around looking puzzled, although my statement must have made as much sense to him as his dialogue had to me. And the third man—the man in the middle, the tallest and broadest and blackest of them all—paused only long enough to register recognition, surprise, and resolution.

Then he moved. One arm lashed out, palm flat and fingers extended, swinging in a sure backhand stroke that caught the standing-around-looking-puzzled man full in the throat. As the blow landed my man was already striding forward, his other hand reaching out to the man with murderous intent. The hand caught a shoulder and spun, and the other hand, no longer busy with the puzzled man's throat, bunched its fingers and stabbed at the midsection, burying itself in the solar plexus and thrusting upward.

All of this happened very quickly while I just stood there and held onto my fork. The man who'd been chopped in the throat made a terrible sound and fell in stages to the ground. His knees buckled, and his body bent at the waist, and he went down as if torpedoed. The other man came right up onto his toes, lifted by the claw in his middle. He made a whooshing sound as air came out of him in a rush, making its exit either from his mouth, which seemed more likely, or through the hole in his belly, which seemed possible at the time. His back was to me so I couldn't really be sure, but either way the air went out of him, and so did the resistance, and so, I guess, did life itself. He flopped onto the floor and stayed there.

And the big man, who had done all of this as easily as he had flung me across the room, said, "You're absolutely right about that, needless to say. Ontogeny certainly does recapitulate phylogeny."

"Every time," I said.

"One never sees phylogeny," he said, "without it's been recapitulated by ontogeny."

Plum was saying, "Wha', wha'—" The two men on the ground were saying nothing at all.

I said, "Sam Bowman."

The big man looked at me. He just stood there looking at me, and then slowly his lips eased into a broad grin, parting to show white teeth. "Yeah," he said, drawling. "Sam Goddamn Bowman himself. And just who in the hell are you, man?"

Introductions didn't take long. When we all knew who we were, it was time to look to the future. The future looked uncertain at best.

Bowman checked the two men on the floor, and they

turned out to be dead, which is what we had assumed. "So much for witnesses," he said cheerfully. "But that ain't the end of the problem. The question, baby, is what we gonna do about you two."

I told him that was simple—we were heading for home and he could join us. He said it wasn't that simple at all.

"Ol' Sheena has her boys strung out all over this patch of real estate, man. We knew you were here last night. If we tried to split now, we wouldn't make a mile without coming up against some of my old buddies."

"Are they that good at combat?"

"You believe it. I trained 'em myself."

"These two didn't give you much trouble."

"Oh, they didn't expect anything, see. They were digging you, and I just came along and zapped them. And then they trusted me, see, which is always a mistake, like." He shook his head. "No chance," he said. "Only thing is to go back to where Sheena is at and pass you off as members of the tribe." He shook his head. "Which ain't gonna be exactly easy. Sellin' you two to Sheena is like sellin' sand in the desert."

"Tell her we're friendly. That we're on her side, something like that."

"You're the wrong color, man. And the bird, she's the wrong sex. You know anything about Sheena? She's one beautiful crazy-ass chick, man. Great big blonde with jugs out to here and wild legs, looks like something out of a Swedish movie."

"Where did she come from?"

"She was a missionary's daughter."

"You're putting me on."

But he wasn't. Sheena, it seemed, had started life as plain Jane Grey ("Unlucky Lady Jane," Bowman said) until a cannibal gang cooked and ate her parents. Jane was on hand to watch all this, and was at a sufficiently impressionable age for the spectacle to leave scars. Additional scars were left by the cannibals' subsequent treatment of Jane herself—they used her to satisfy another hunger entirely, raping her beyond the bounds of good taste.

One might think that this sort of treatment would have made Jane, who had been shy anyway, and who had experienced a typically repressed childhood, into a man-fearing black-hating desiccated old bitch, and perhaps a vegetarian in the bargain. But somehow the Fates turned the picture inside out and printed it as a negative. She hated whites, not blacks. She hated women, not men. Far from desiccated, she was genuinely juicy, a full-fledged polyandrous nymphomaniac. (These—mark it well—are my words. Bowman's description was less scholarly.)

Nor was she any sort of vegetarian. I learned now what had happened to the various human organs the absence of which I had last night noted. They had been eaten.

"So you see where it's at," he summed up. "Certain people don't get to live when Sheena has any say about it. Like all women, white or black. And like all white men. And like any black men who won't come join the harem. Which comes out"—he sighed—"that we got a problem. You're white. The chick is half-white and also she's a chick."

Plum snorted quietly.

"Not that I'm complainin' myself, understand." He beamed at her, and her irritation dissolved in the glow of the smile. "Wouldn't have you any other way, baby. That mixed-blood bag is very exotic. I dig it."

I think she blushed.

"Thing is, you can't come into Sheena's camp looking like yourselves. But there's a way around it. There generally is, has been my experience. We cut your hair short enough and darken it up some and it won't look so bloody Caucasian. Use some dyes to darken your face. Darken up the bird's, too, and her hair. At least it's kinky to start with. Makes it easier."

"I knew it would come in handy someday," Plum said.

"Have to tie them there up a little," he went on, pointing at her breasts. "And Evan, my man, I don't guess it would hurt for you to join the red crotch club. It's just this cochineal dye she has us put on. Don't hurt none, and to tell you the truth I think it keeps the flies off."

"What about Plum?"

"She have much trouble with flies?"

"No, but—"

"No point then, man."

This stupidity got sorted out when Bowman explained that Sheena and her Merry Men only went naked on selected occasions, such as massacres, so that they wouldn't get blood on their clothing. He and his two erstwhile buddies had been fully dressed when they came calling on us, but had stripped outside and left the clothes there. We could even wear their clothes, he suggested; it might help make the deception effective.

I don't know if it did or not, really. In Plum's case, the white duck slacks were a foot and a half too long for her, the waist almost that much too large for her, and the canvas tunic was so oversized that her breasts disappeared in it; there was really no point in binding them. My outfit came a little closer to my size—either my opponent had been less gigantic than he had seemed or the clothes had been too small for him.

We had no sooner gotten the clothes on than we took them off again and began making ourselves over as members of Sheena's gang. Bowman took charge of things, and I was more than happy to let him. I had lost the ability for intelligent planning somewhere along the way and didn't know if I would ever get it back. It was easier by far to nod and grunt while my hair got shortened and my skin darkened and my generative paraphernalia dyed a screaming scarlet.

He did the honors for Miss Pelham Jenkins, too. I had to admit that the transformation was fairly remarkable. The little bridge of freckles disappeared as her skin turned several shades darker. The very unusual cap of blond curls became a very usual cap of dark brown curls. Sam Bowman did good work, and if it seemed to me that his hands lingered rather too affectionately on the flesh he was darkening, there was really nothing I was entitled to do or say about it.

And through it all, Bowman talked. About the life he had for himself, roaming the jungles with Sheena's gang and instructing them in hand-to-hand combat and guerrilla warfare techniques. About his flight from

Griggstown, and how he had been very nearly killed a dozen times, and how he would have starved to death or died of a fever if he hadn't met up with Sheena. About the Chief, and the stupidity of this assignment, and the superiority of the average urban ghetto to the average jungle, and of the average urban ghetto dweller to the average denizen of the bush.

"Not that these cats don't have a certain charm, you dig. Because they do. And they are purely beautiful at getting their bodies to do what their heads tell them. When I was in Oakland with the Panthers we would get all these very straight college boys stuffed up to here with Black Power slogans. All hung up on Afro culture and Mao and Che, the whole bag. Intense, you know. I'd lay some judo and karate on them and they'd practice day and night and concentrate on nothing else, but it was like their bodies wasn't right for it. They didn't feel it, they didn't have the rhythm for it, and they never did get it down right."

I asked about Knanda Ndoro, and about the details of his assignment. He said he had been sent to rescue the Retriever but was rather bitterly surprised when I let him know that America had simultaneously supported the side that deposed the dictator. "They never told me that," he said.

"Maybe they wanted to make your performance more convincing."

"They do one thing with one hand and the opposite thing with the other."

"The other hand was the CIA."

"What's the difference?"

"Well, it's part of the policy of competing brands. They learned it from Procter and Gamble."

He didn't seem amused at this. He thought it over and just shook his head, and I asked again what had happened to Ndoro.

"Knanda Ndoro," he said. "The Modonoland Retriever. Quite a man, Tanner cat. Quite a man. Know much about him?"

"Not much," I said.

"He was a fascist bastard," Plum said.

Bowman seemed not to have heard. His face took on an odd quality. "A natural leader," he said. "An infinitely charismatic man. A charmer. Tremendous natural intelligence, a good British education, and enormous personal magnetism. Maybe he was bad for the country in some ways, but he was damned good for it in others. Gave these buggers a sense of identity, a feeling of national purpose.

"I had a hard time getting him to leave the capital. He wanted to stay. Of course we got out at the last minute. You must know about that. Then that mad rush through the jungle. I thought we were clear at one point. I thought the two of us, you know, would be equal to anything the jungle might throw up against us."

He lowered his eyes and dropped his voice. "Then the fever struck. I caught it first and came close to dying. But he nursed me through it. And then, just as I was recovering nicely, he came down with it. He was burning up with fever and couldn't eat and was delirious and, oh, it was terrible." A pulse worked in his temple. "I stayed up with him day and night. I tried to bring him out of it by sheer force of will, but my will just wasn't equal to that fever. After three days and nights of it he died.

"I dug his grave with my own two hands. By the side of a tree near a river bank. Scooped out the dirt with my own two hands and laid him to rest. I thought of a poem they taught me in school. Stevenson wrote it, Robert Louis Stevenson, for his own epitaph. It went like this:

> *Under a wide and starry sky,*
> *Dig my grave and let me lie.*
> *Glad did I live and gladly die,*
> *And I laid me down with a will.*

> *This be the verse you grave for me:*
> *Here he lies where he longed to be;*
> *Home is the sailor, home from sea*
> *And the hunter home from the hill.*

"I thought that might make a good epitaph for him, that it was fitting. But I had nothing to write with and nothing to write on, and anyway I knew I'd never be able to mark that grave so I could find it again. So what was the point of an epitaph if wasn't anybody going to know who was buried there? What I did was I just spoke the words aloud, and I don't suppose that did any more good than writin' them, but it was something to do and I did it."

He heaved a sigh, and we were all three respectfully silent for a few moments. "He must have been a very great man," Plum said. A few moments ago, I seemed to recall, she had characterized the late Retriever as a fascist bastard. Women are decidedly fickle.

Bowman agreed that the Retriever had indeed been a great man. "You hear all these people talk about Black Power," he said, "and here's a guy actually went and did something about it. And with such style, such flair."

"You must have been terribly devoted to him," she said.

"Well, I could say it was just a job. Just the same old shuck." He grinned gently. "But I'll tell you a thing as straight as anything anybody ever told you, Plum kitten. And that's that nobody on earth was ever as devoted to anybody as I was to Knanda Ndoro. And that's the truth."

Plum bowed her head and closed her eyes. Bowman let the poetic beauty of the scene build to a peak, then borrowed my Swiss Army pocketknife to scalp his two former comrades. *Scalp* is not the right word for it, but it will have to do. There was still some alcohol in my jug, and we used it to wash the red dye from the, uh, scalps. They would be presented to Sheena, who would accept them as trophies of the hunt even as she accepted Plum and me as faithful members of her rebel band. At least that was the theory.

I pictured Bowman digging Knanda Ndoro's grave with his own two hands. I wanted to ask him about the treasure, but it seemed inappropriate to bring it up now.

Chapter 10

"And the voice of the Lord came unto Jane, and spake unto her. And the Lord said, Lo, thou art white, and thy father was white and his father before him. And the whiteness of thy father and thy father's father is an abomination in my eyes, and thou art whitened as a sepulcher. So henceforth shalt thy name not be Jane, but from this day forward and forevermore shalt thou be called Sheena, which means Queen of the Jungle.

"And the voice of the Lord spake unto Jane called Sheena, and said unto her, Lo, over every living thing shalt thou have dominion, over them that groweth in the ground and them that creepeth in the sky and them that lieth down and them that riseth up. And over every man and every woman shalt thou have dominion, and of the men, if they be white, then shalt they surely be put to death. And of the women, if they be black or white, they shall be surely put to death. And of the men, if they be black, let them come into thy tent, and let them lie with thee, and let them come unto thee when thou liest down and when thou risest up.

"And the voice of the Lord—"

I tuned out the voice of the Lord, no disrespect intended, and let my eyes take over for my ears. Sheena was a far cry better to look at than to listen to. As far as the eyes were concerned, she was a *Playboy* centerfold brought miraculously to life, the ideal Playmate of this or any other month. She had hair so golden the French peasantry would have hoarded it and eyes as blue as a Billie Holiday record. Her breasts convinced one that mammals were God's chosen creatures, and that God had the right idea. Her legs went all the way up to her neck.

The ears received another message entirely. If she looked like a wet dream, she sounded like Cotton Mather on an acid trip. She ran down the gospel according to St. Sheena with the precise cadence of a New England preacher. I was occasionally reminded of the Book of Mormon; the Angel Moroni, like Sheena, had tended to transmit his revelations in King James English. And, also like Sheena, he had frequently made less than an abundance of sense. It kept sounding right, but it kept not meaning anything.

Actually, she might almost as well have been reciting the Book of Mormon, or the Magna Carta, or the Rime of the Ancient Mariner, or the Complete Works of Chester Alan Arthur, for all the impression it was making on her disciples. They evidently liked the sound of it, and the sound of it was all they got, because Sheena was babbling on and on in English— albeit her own personal version thereof—and of all the crowd gathered around her, only Plum and Bowman and I understood English. The rest of them—of us—could no more understand English than I could understand them.

I drew Sam aside and asked him if Sheena spoke the native language. "Just English," he said. "I don't think she understands the native tongue, either. And they don't understand her. It's a very heavy relationship."

"What language do the natives speak?"

"I don't know the name of it. I can get around in it without breaking a leg, but I don't know what you'd call it. Some local dialect. It's nothing like what they speak farther south."

"How does Sheena talk to the men?"

"You're hearing her."

"I mean how does she communicate?"

"Through me, now. She'll tell me something in English and I'll translate it into wog-gabble. I don't know how she worked it before I happened on. But dig, it's weird. They always seem to know what she has in mind. Like I tried turning her orders upside down one day, and it didn't take. She has this fantastic intuitive thing with them. A very down scene. She doesn't tell them what to do so much as she does things, she gets into a set, and they act in concert with her." He shook his head in reminiscence. "The best illustration is at a massacre. The lady's at her best at a massacre. She doesn't tell anybody what to do. She just wades right in and lets fly, reelin' off her own personal scripture and swingin' that machete of hers like the jawbone of an ass. When we raid a village or wipe out a mission, she is purely beautiful."

"You sound as though you enjoy it."

"Shit, man, who wouldn't?" His eyes met mine. "It's all the same scrum, baby. Whether it's Oakland cops or back-country priests and nuns, it's the same ofay establishment. It's cuttin' whitey up and makin' him bleed, that's what it's all about. After four hundred years of slavery, you got to expect a little desire for vengeance."

I must have backed off, or looked as though I was about to, because all at once the tension and fervor left his face and his features eased into a grin. "Nothing personal, Tanner cat. Course you understand that."

"Sure," I said, unsure.

"Just a matter of *not* cuttin' off your hose despite your race, is how you maybe could put it. One white man is one thing. I can dig you on a personal level. But in the abstract, the whole lot of you, that's somethin' else."

"But missionaries," I said. "Priests and nuns, doctors and nurses. I don't—"

"Missionaries!" He shouted the word, and several nearby warriors turned to gape at us. I tried to shrink away from them and avoid their eyes. My makeup job was fairly good, but the closer one looked at me the whiter I appeared. "Motherfucking bloodyminded missionaries," he went on, in a lower register now. "Tanner cat, those are the worstest white devils of all. No question, no argument. Give me the straight-out colonialist any day of the week. You know where you stand with him. Like the Mississippi sheriff—he may kill you, but he won't lay a load of bullshit on you. But the missionary, he comes into my country where I got my own religion and my own way of doing things, my own ceremonies and costumes and medicine and agriculture, and he gives out some vaccinations and passes around some food, and the next thing you know he's sayin' how my religion is a shuck and my ceremonies are a crock and my medicine's a superstition and my crops don't grow right, and what he's tryin' to do is turn me into a white man on the inside and leave me the same old bush nigger outside. The colonialist takes a man's body and leaves him his soul, and that's bad, but it's a damn sight worse the other way around. That whole missionary attitude, that holier-than-thou routine, that white man's burden birdsong. I hate that, man. It makes me want to reach out and rip things."

And again the eyes were blazing, the forehead creased, the veins standing out on the glossy black temples. And again, too, the passion waned all at once and teeth flashed in a smile. "Course you wouldn't buy that," he said.

"No, I agree. Missionaries are the most arrogant people in the world, and they don't even know it, they actually think they're humble. But—"

"But you don't buy killing them."

"Not especially, no."

"Because their hearts are pure, right?"

"Not exactly that, but—"

He clapped me on the shoulder. It was a friendly gesture but one that very nearly knocked me from my feet. "Tanner cat, the trouble with you, you know what it is?"

"I'm white."

"Well, that's maybe part of it. But you can't help it, it's just an accident at birth. The sort of thing that's apt to happen to a man when both his parents is white. The real trouble is that you just aren't a fanatic."

The Federal Bureau of Investigation, which checks my mail, thinks I'm a fanatic. The Central Intelligence Agency, which bugs my apartment, concurs in this judgment. The police of countries all over the globe, having spotted my name on lists of various unwelcome organizations, concur in the opinion. I'm not even allowed in Canada, and you can't be a whole hell of a lot more fanatic than that.

But that wild-eyed fanatic was the *old* Evan Tanner. And if the leopard can change his spots and the Nixon his image, surely the Tanner can mature from youthful fanaticism to mature responsibility. And, I thought now, in my new role of Scarsdale Galahad and Levittown Lochinvar, in my chosen identity of breakfast-eating Brooks Brothers type, I couldn't deny the truth of Samuel Lonestar Bowman's remark. I just wasn't a fanatic.

A little later I repeated most of the conversation with Plum. She didn't concur in Bowman's opinion of missionaries. As far as she was concerned, no one who fed the hungry, clothed the naked, and healed the sick could be all bad. Her trouble was that she wasn't a fanatic either.

"And they don't just kill white people," she pointed out. "They kill black people as well. There were black corpses at the mission."

"I know. When they hit a mission, they kill everything that moves."

"And when they raid the villages, they do not merely do this to get supplies and to recruit more men for their forces. They kill and loot and burn."

"True."

"And they kill all women, Evan. Not just white women. Black women as well."

"True. That's Sheena's idea. It's a particular fixation she has. She wants to be the only woman in the world."

"Honestly?"

"So Bowman says. There's no one else I can ask."

"That's some ambition of hers."

"It's every woman's ambition, deep down inside. It's just that she's doing more to achieve it than most."

"If someone does not do something, Evan, she may manage it."

"It doesn't seem too likely."

"But Evan," she said, her hand on my arm. "Listen to me. You have said how Bowman likes to kill white men, and his reasons, and I think the reasons are crazy but I can understand why he might feel this way. But what about the harmless villagers? And all of the black women? Why should he be willing to kill them?"

I covered her hand with mine, then let go abruptly and glanced hurriedly around. No one seemed to have noticed, and Plum looked oddly at me. I told her that everybody thought she was a boy, and that if we held hands and necked the other clowns would either figure out that she was female, in which case she would get the ax, or assume that I was some kind of a faggot. I wasn't quite sure how tribesmen in the Modonoland interior felt about homosexuality. While it seemed the sort of thing worth knowing, I felt it might be just as well to wait until I was back in New York and then look it up in an anthropological journal. Sometimes second-hand research has its points.

But I didn't dwell on this, and Plum took her hand off my arm, and I reminded myself that, from here on in, she might as well be a boy for all I cared. We'd had our last fling. It was time to be faithful to Kitty.

"Getting back to Bowman," I said, by way of getting back to Bowman. "He's a fairly arresting type, don't you think? An extremely charming type. He can chill your blood one minute and take it all back with a smile."

"He talks weird."

"I know. He shifts back and forth from Harlem hard-bop jive to plantation hand to college graduate. Sometimes he even sounds vaguely British. It goes along with being a good linguist, which he damned well must be to handle the dialect they speak here. It sounds like turkey. Not the country, the bird. You know—gobble gobble."

"I don't trust him, Evan."

"Neither do I. But we can't really get out of here without his help—we can't even survive without it. And he can't get away without us."

"How do you know?"

"He's been here a long while now and never got away so far."

"Maybe he wants to stay." Her lip curled and her eyes looked older by some years. "Maybe your friend Bowman likes it here."

"He doesn't want to stay. He can stand it here, all right, but it won't keep him happy for very long. He's too complex to settle for the Noble Savage routine."

"I suppose you are right. I know that he has depth. When he spoke of the death of the Retriever, even while I knew the political crimes of Knanda Ndoro, yet I was moved, Evan."

"Well, he's charming. And he's complex, and he has depth, and I know damned well he has a use for us or else he would have killed us back at the mission. Because it's not hard to say why Bowman goes along with killing innocent blacks and their women. I think he just plain enjoys it."

The Red Ball Irregulars were just another army, after all. And armies are armies as sure as war is hell, and this one, like the one I had served in (and like the one Napoleon served in, and like the one Julius Caesar served in) was an organization of hurry up and wait, a group which spent most of its collective time doing nothing at all.

We spent the rest of that day doing nothing at all. Sheena had pitched camp on the site of an abandoned village about a dozen miles from the ruined mission. The abandonment of the village had not been entirely voluntary; several months previously Sheena had raided it, and its huts were subsequently unoccupied because of the demise of the previous occupants. The jungle had made a good start at reclaiming the cleared land, and weather had done a job on the huts, but they were still standing and reasonably sound. Plum and I had one all to ourselves, and we spent most of the day sitting in it and grunting at each other.

The others, forty or fifty of them, spent most of their time sharpening knives and machetes, practicing hand-to-hand combat, combing their ancillary hair for lice, picking their noses, and scratching themselves. In the interests of verisimilitude I tried to be doing one or more of these things whenever anyone was looking my way. The only knife I had was distinctly out of place in that company, and if I got involved in their hand-to-hand contests the game would be up in no time at all, so that left lice hunting, nose picking, and general scratching. I didn't mind hunting for lice, but I was more than a little disconcerted when I began finding them. I tried to console myself with the thought that this lent additional verisimilitude to the pose. This was relatively little consolation.

Shortly before sunset, they began preparing for the feast. Men piled mountains of brush and planks from a dilapidated hut in the center of the village and poured a can of some petroleum distillate on it. One of them struck a match—looting does provide one with the trappings of civilization—and the whole thing went up in a glorious whooshing blaze.

They let the fire burn down, then heaped more

brush and boards on it and let them flame up and burn down until there was a deep bed of fiery coals. By this time the sun had dropped behind the trees and the glow of the campfire was the only available light. Three men carried a huge cast-iron kettle and set it atop the bed of coals. Various men began throwing things into the kettle. This went on for quite some time. Then Sheena came out of her quarters and said something which sounded like a remake of the Book of Judges, a section dealing with a triumph given for Samson, I think. It was hard to be sure. It was even harder to guess what she had in mind, but the general gist of it was that the warriors of the Lord could not rest on their laurels but must move from victory through the fruits of triumph to a fresh engagement with the enemy. There was an all-purpose feel to it, and it didn't differ much in content from what Vince Lombardi used to tell the Packers the morning after they won a close one.

Bowman said a few words after that, but I could no more understand him than the others could tell what Sheena meant. I hate not being able to understand what someone else is saying. I really find it unendurable. It's a situation I don't face very often, and it was consequently particularly maddening.

After his speech, the Gray Panther followed Sheena into her shack and the chefs let the caldron bubble for a spell. I was squatting on my haunches in the doorway of our hut, and Plum came up and squatted beside me. Cooking smells wafted in our direction, and I said that it smelled very good indeed, which indeed it did.

"What do you suppose it is?"

"Oh, all different things," I said. I had managed to identify some of the ingredients as they found their way into the pot. "They evidently massacred the mission livestock along with the human beings. A couple of hens went into the pot, and what must have been a goat or a sheep, and I think a hog. Plus a variety of fruits and vegetables. Some roots that looked like parsnips, although I suppose they could have been almost anything."

"Almost anything," she echoed.

"We're both starving, all right. That food is going to taste damned good, Plum."

"Damned good."

"Nothing to eat since I can't remember when. Except for the eggs, and you remember what a failure they were. Pretty horrible, huh?"

"Pretty horrible."

"But from the smell, this stew or whatever you want to call it, it should be great. You must be hungry as a bear, huh? You didn't even keep the eggs down, so you must be just about ready to faint from hunger. I'll tell you, when they bring that stew around, it's going to taste like a banquet."

"Like a banquet."

I looked at her. "Why do you keep repeating everything I say?"

"Because I am trying to believe you, Evan, almost as hard as you are trying to convince me. But it is not working out properly."

"Why not?"

"Because we both know what is in that stew."

"Pork and lamb and chicken, and what's so bad about that? Nothing wrong with pork and lamb and chicken, is there? Oh, maybe it wasn't lamb, maybe it was goat, and maybe you've never eaten goat, but it's as good as lamb if not better. They call it chevon, which is a handy word if the thought of eating goat bothers you. What the hell, different people eat different things all over the world." I was talking rapidly now, and my voice hadn't been this high since it changed a couple of decades ago. "The Chinese eat dogs, did you know that? Young puppies are considered a great delicacy there. They also eat monkeys. Sounds terrible, but *de gustibus* and all that. Goat, now—"

"Evan, you know I am not talking about goat."

"Er."

"I am sure there are all the things you said in that stew, but I am sure there are also parts of human beings."

"Uh."

"The parts that had been removed."

"Umm."

"So do not talk of goats."

"Plum, we have to eat." She made a face. "I know, I know, but we have to eat. We can't let ourselves starve to death." She went on making a face. "Well, look at it another way. I mean, how do you know you won't like it? Remember the fuss you made about the dead antelope? Couldn't stand the idea of eating it, you said.

It was dead meat, meat just lying there on the ground, you said. Unrefrigerated, probably teeming with bacteria, you said. But once you tasted it—"

"Evan, please stop it."

"You can't starve yourself."

"Human beings fast for a month or more without harming themselves. They gain religious insight and learn important truths."

"The most important truth they learn is that eating is good for you."

"That is not true, Evan." She tossed her head. "I am not eating any of that."

"You could just pick out bits of vegetable—"

"I am not eating. I am not hungry. I am tired, Evan, and I think I will lie down and go to sleep before it is discovered that I am neither black nor a man." Her eyes welled with tears. "You were right."

"About what?"

"When you told me I should stay in Griggstown." All at once she threw her arms around my neck and sobbed.

"Oh, I'm afraid," she said. "I am truly afraid."

When she was asleep I slipped out of the hut and joined the crowd. The feast was getting into gear now, with the stew almost ready for serving. The young bloods were starting to tank up on a home-brewed malty liquor, and when someone passed me a gourd of it I didn't pass it back. It smelled of moldy bread and spoiled fruit, but the taste wasn't bad and the stuff had a reasonable kick to it. It couldn't compare to the grain alcohol of the night before, which was probably just as well. I refilled my gourd a few times and mingled with my fellow soldiers, scratching and picking my nose and grunting amiably at them. I thought I looked like a short-haired white man who had stained his skin with roots and berries, but if they thought as much they were good enough to keep it to themselves. They didn't even seem to notice my ignorance of their language. Every once in a while I would say *"Banana Kropotkin Pulaski,"* a phrase I kept hearing others use, and I guess it was always appropriate, because no one took a swing at me.

Of course the fact that they were all stoned out of their gourds may have helped a little.

Somewhere along the way I set the gourd aside and accepted a plate heaped high with stew. I had been drinking not only because I wanted to but also with the thought in mind that the stew would be easier to take after a couple of belts, and now I tried it, and it was great. I guess there was human flesh in it. When all is said and done, I don't think there's any way to avoid that conclusion. I've tried rationalizing my way out of it often enough, God knows, but it won't hold up. There was human flesh in that fine kettle of flesh, and I ate a heaping plateful of crud served from that kettle, ate it without picking it over, ate it unselectively and voraciously, and the argument that I might well have actually consumed nothing more unorthodox than pork and chicken and lamb (or chevon) is pure sophistry.

They were never going to believe this in Paramus.

*   *   *

Once I had finished with my food I let myself withdraw from the party. The festive mood had not quite caught hold of me, and I was afraid that another gourd of punch would make me lose my cool. I went back to my hut to check on Plum. She was still sleeping, and from the tenor of her breathing she was sleeping well, untroubled by nightmares. I wished her well and stretched out beside her for a few moments of rest. I went through the full cycle of relaxation exercises, all of which were easier on a full stomach and with a modicum of alcohol in my system. Certain muscle groups were stubborn—the eyelids, the solar plexus area, the calf of my left leg, each of them showing a persistent propensity for tightening up of their own accord. But I managed to unwind fairly well, and when I packed it in after a half hour or so and yawned and stretched and yawned again and sat up, I was better rested than I had been in a couple of days.

Outside, the party was just getting into top form. The bloody minded cannibals were dancing up a storm. They had discarded their clothing, and their red genitals flashed in the firelight. There seemed to be a limitless supply of the malt liquor, and it seemed to have a far greater effect upon them than it had on me. Every once in a while one of them would go rigid and fall over as if he had been clubbed. His fellows would leave him where he lay, and he would just stay there without moving anything.

It occurred to me, and not for the first time, that this would have been an ideal time for the three of us to get the hell out of there. I had been thinking this ever since they trotted out the booze, and the more the red crotch set drank, the more sense the idea made to me. But Bowman was still in Sheena's hut, and there were two sober guards in front of that hut, and Plum was asleep, and we hadn't made plans, and it looked as though we would have to put it off for a day or two. Not for too long, though, because judging from the familiarity my cannibal friends were displaying out there, feasts were not that unusual a part of army life. It looked as though they did this sort of thing rather often.

I did slip outside three or four times looking for Bowman, but it was no use. The first few times the sentry was doing his job and I couldn't even get close to Sheena's hut. The final time I got to it and inside it, and I called Bowman's name a few times and got no response whatsoever. He seemed to be asleep, so I gave it up and went back to Plum. Now and then she would make a frightened noise and I would soothe her back to gentler sleep.

I was in the doorway at sunup when Bowman left Sheena's tent and staggered across the central clearing, weaving his way through a maze of inert human forms. I gave him a wave and he came over and dropped to the ground, breathing very heavily. "Shee-it," he said. "That woman ought to be outlawed. I never thought I'd live to have so much I wouldn't want any more, but the day has done come. I know how Samson felt when he got that haircut. Maybe it wasn't his hair they cut. You ever think of it that way?"

"Yes."

"You did?" He shrugged, disappointed. I said something about how nice it would have been if we could have gotten the hell out of there that night, what with all of the others stoned. "Yeah, but we get another chance in two days," he said. "There's a party after every raid, and there's a raid comin' up tomorrow."

"Another one?"

He scratched a map in the dirt. "She laid it all on me in between the acts. We're here now. This here is the Yellowfoot River. It swings up and then winds down and out, and it's the very same Yellowfoot that you followed north from Griggstown."

"We followed the highway. That brilliant road the Retriever built."

"Beautiful, ain't it? You got to give the man credit." He smiled and clicked his tongue. "Dig it, this here's the Yellowfoot, and right at the top of this bend is the leprosarium. We break camp in a couple of hours and head for the river and get ourselves some boats, and then we—"

"The what?"

"The leprosarium, Tanner cat. Like a hospital for people with leprosy."

"I know what a leprosarium is, for Christ's sake."

"Well, don't get shirty, man. You asked so I told you. The idea is we spend today getting ready and tomorrow we hit the place sometime in the afternoon. We'll be headin' downstream, so that takes the pressure off. It ain't all that far anyway. We hit the leprosarium—"

"Wait a minute. We hit the leprosarium? We kill doctors and nurses and, God help them, lepers?"

"That's the drill, baby." He furrowed his brow, scratched his head. "I get your drift, Tanner cat. I truly do."

"Great."

"I do. It don't seem right, killing the lepers, wrecking the leprosarium. It don't seem right at all." He sighed mightily. "But to tell you the truth, I don't see what choice we got open. We maybe can escape when the right time comes, but we sure can't manage it now. And tomorrow's the day we hit the lepers. So what else we gonna do?"

*C*hapter 11

*F*at black flies buzzed in the reeds that lined the riverbank. Bees worried the trumpet-shaped blood-hued blossoms of a puri-puri vine, which in turn worried the trunk of a stately wali tree. To our right, one of the younger members of the company flipped pebbles into the sluggish brown water.

I squatted and explored myself for lice. I felt as sluggish and brown as the Yellowfoot River. It was noon, and it was hot, and after a rough morning's march to the river we were playing the usual game of hurry up and wait. I stifled a yawn and scratched an itch and tried to remember what coffee tasted like.

Bowman was giving Plum a hard time. "You sure do look like a boy," I heard him say, "but I know better, don't I? Because I had a long uninterrupted look at you at that mission, Plum kitten, and that wasn't no boy I was lookin' at."

I don't know whether Plum blushed or blanched or what. It was impossible to tell beneath the coloring.

"And I sure did like your color, Plum kitten. Earl Grey tea with sweet cream in it. That's rare, that combination. Black is beautiful, but brown can stick around when it looks like you."

Plum looked extremely uncomfortable. He was bugging her, and she didn't like it, but at the same time she wasn't prepared to reply sharply or get up and walk away. He had that effect on people. And I suppose, too, that in part she gloried in the flattery. It would have been extraordinary if she hadn't.

I found it annoying, and not merely out of simple jealousy combined with my own protective feelings toward the girl. These factors were there, but so was the conviction that our situation called for more urgent matters than verbal seduction. In less than twenty-four hours we were scheduled to participate in an act of barbarism unparalleled in our experience and unexceeded in human history. The idea of depriving a gaggle of wretched lepers of their few remaining organs was utterly appalling. And the knowledge that every passing hour increased the likelihood that we, too, would be similarly deprived did nothing much for my state of mind either.

I said, "Look, we just don't have time to waste. We have to cut out of here before that raid."

"Can't be done, Tanner cat."

"It has to be done."

"During, maybe. If we run into a little resistance at the leper place there might be enough going on so that the three of us could shove one of the dugouts back into the water and get clear before they knew we were gone. Not much chance the lepers will put up a big fight though, is there? Some of the staff will have guns for defense against animals, but the way this gang fights they'll be out of the play before they get to their guns, and what are the lepers goin' to do? Beat us off with their stumps? No, tomorrow night's the time. Everybody be drunk and passed out, and we can slip a boat into the river and be miles away before they know we're gone."

"Why can't we do that tonight?"

"No chance."

"Why not?"

"Because they won't be drinking tonight, man. And when they don't drink they don't do anything sloppy." He let out a long sigh. "Used to be different before I came along. They would all sleep at once, didn't even post a single damned sentry. I changed all that. Taught 'em to post a dozen men at a time on two-hour watches. They ring the whole camp and keep in touch with bird-call hoots."

"You taught them that, did you?"

He nodded.

"And taught them to fight dirty."

"Well, if you can't lick 'em, you join 'em."

"There's a difference between joining them and turning them into a professional army." I closed my eyes and tried to concentrate, opening them at the sound of a giggle and a slap. Plum had giggled, and Bowman had been slapped. I did my best to ignore this.

I said, "All right. We've got to make our move tonight. It may not be as hard as you think. For one thing, they don't expect anything. I don't mean to be critical, but these troops of yours don't seem geared for long-range planning, Sam. They aren't the thinking type."

"True. They live in the moment."

"In the now. Exactly. Which means that it might be difficult to take them with a headlong rush or a sudden surprise attack, but that calculated subterfuge might have a chance."

"In other words," said Plum, "we con them."

"Or in still better words," said Bowman, "we think white. We fake out the trusting natives when they least expect it."

He sounded bitter. "Maybe it offends your black pride," I said, "but try to live with it. These are desperate times. After all, the odds are something like fifty to three."

"Two."

"Huh?"

"Fifty to two," Bowman said. "You won't be playing."

"I don't follow you."

"Well, she told me last night, man, but I was saving it for a surprise. Sheena, man. Like Uncle Sam in all them recruitin' posters. She wants you."

I blinked.

"Tonight," he said, grinning pleasantly. "You and Sheena, Tanner cat. It's your turn in the barrel."

An hour before sundown Samuel Lonestar Bowman and I made our way over a stretch of reasonably clear ground to the site where Sheena's tent was pitched. Two sentries crouched out in front. They reminded me of the lions at the New York Public Library. One of them was whittling a branch. His knife had a sharply curved blade, and looked menacing. The other also held a knife. The blade was longer and straighter, and he wasn't carving anything with it. He was just holding it and looking dangerous.

Bowman spoke to the carver, reeling off several ornate sentences of gibberish. The sentry did not appear at first to have heard. He went on whittling for a few moments. Then he straightened up abruptly, put down the hunk of wood, and tucked a knife into the waistband of his trousers. He went into Sheena's tent. The other sentry contrived to look twice as menacing as usual in order to take up the slack.

The carver reappeared wordlessly, dropped to a crouch, picked up the chunk of wood, and whipped out his knife. He resumed carving, ignoring us completely. This was evidently his way of approving our credentials. Alone I might have been a little diffident about brushing on past him, but Sam led the way and I only had to follow.

Inside, a candle glowed to illuminate the interior of the tent. It was more spacious than I would have guessed, and far more elaborately appointed. When you considered that the tent was a mobile unit, taken up when the troupe broke camp and pitched anew when the day's march ended, it seemed surprisingly comfortable. It was light-tight, and it had room enough for a lush bed of straw and leaves on which our matriarch was doing her supine white goddess number. Her platinum-gold hair cascaded over bare shoulders. Animal skins covered her breasts and lower body. One leg was extended, the other doubled up, as in Italian paintings of orgiastic pagan deities.

Bowman said, "This be Tanner, who comes to be husband to Sheena, Queen of the Jungle and hope of heaven." He bowed his head. "What God has laid together, let no man put asunder." He said a few more words, bowed again, and backed out of the tent.

I had been well coached, and knew my part. I dropped to one knee beside her, genuflected, got to my feet. I shucked off the shapeless cotton shirt and trousers and stood naked for her inspection. We had renewed the body make-up with fresh roots and berries, and I had collected a handful of cochineal beetles which supplied the red dye. The candle provided imperfect light, and Sheena squinted to study me.

I felt my stomach muscles tighten, felt a pulse working in my throat. This was the crucial moment. Bowman was waiting outside, ready to spring into action if the thing blew up in our faces. With luck I might be able to cool Sheena before she sounded the alarm, and we might have a chance to make a desperate break. But if she didn't tip now, our odds improved hearteningly.

"She's right on top of things at the beginning," Bowman had told me. "There's a first-rate mind underneath all the flakiness, and now and then she can use it. But if she doesn't make you as white right off the bat, you could be home free. Because after she performs the marriage ceremony, she gets involved in consummating it, and she's got a real genius for consummation. She gets all involved in what she's doing. Once she's in the swing of things she wouldn't know if she was being humped by a white man or a black man or a donkey. She works a man half to death, but you don't want to think it's all a burden. There are things about that woman I am going to miss a whole lot. But I don't want to spoil it for you, Tanner cat. You just go and have yourself a time."

The trouble was that I didn't feel like having myself a time. If I had felt any less virile I would have sat down and written regional fiction for *The New Yorker*. It struck me that if I passed inspection I would just fail the road test anyway. And that would knock the props out from under our escape plan.

Sheena's eyes scanned me. I waited, and she nodded slowly, and it seemed that I had passed inspection. She seemed neither wildly delighted with what she saw nor abysmally depressed. She motioned with one hand, and I sank again to my knees.

She said, "And thou shalt love the Goddess with all thy heart and with all thy soul and with all thy might. And these words which I command thee this evening shall guide thy spirit all the length of thy days. And thou shall write them upon the doorposts of thy house, and shall make them as a sign in blood upon thy loins. And thou shalt—"

It went on like this, the ceremony did, and while none of it made very much literal sense I couldn't shake the feeling that I had heard it all before, part here and part there. Now and then I recognized a part from the standard marriage ritual, and ultimately we did reach the nitty-gritty:

"Do you, Tanner, take this woman, Sheena, as your bride and goddess, to love, honor, and obey, in sickness and in health, for better or for worse, until death do you in?"

"Katanga Salami Nokomis."

"Then by the authority vested in me I do proclaim us woman and husband. Sticks and stones shall break thy bones but names shall never hurt thee." She shrugged off the pelts, exposing her naked flesh. Her body was so flawlessly formed and so lushly designed it seemed incredible that she did not fold into three parts, that her navel was indeed unstapled. She was honestly too good to be true, and the effect was perversely anaphrodisiacal—that which was so perfectly designed to turn one on had the effect of turning one (more precisely, me) off.

This may reveal a tragic flaw in my own character. I'm not sure. I seem to be encumbered with an unwillingness to believe in the ideal when I encounter it. Spectacular scenery makes me feel that I am watching a film or examining a picture postcard. When I see an extraordinary hairdo I assume the lady is wearing a wig. Plants growing luxuriantly appear plastic. It has occurred to me that this inability to accept perfection may be a corollary to the idea of a man's reach properly exceeding his grasp. And I would have liked to pursue the thought further, but I had other things to contend with.

Sheena, for example.

"Dearly beloved," she was saying, "we have come to bury Caesar, not to praise him. Dust thou art, to dust returneth, and may God have mercy on your soul. You may fuck the bride."

Outside, I knew, Plum and Bowman were getting ready to go into their acts. For simplicity's sake, we had divided the task of escape into three parts, like

Gaul. It was Plum's job to incapacitate about a dozen long dugout canoes, the entire navy of Sheena's entire army. It was Bowman's job to incapacitate somewhere in the neighborhood of fifty men, and it was my job to incapacitate Sheena herself. By any sort of logical analysis, my job was the easiest of the three.

I would have traded even with either of them.

I was still kneeling there, and thinking about this, when Sheena repeated her last sentence. There was a note of irritation in her tone. I had missed my cue, and she didn't seem to like it. It seemed to me that this must happen rather often, since Bowman and I were alone among her husbands in being able to understand what she was saying. I guess the others were good at nonverbal communication and simply did what came naturally.

Time to go to work, I reminded myself. Nice work if you can get it, I told myself. Plenty of trouble if you can't get it, I added. Up.

I reached for the bride.

Chapter 12

It was method acting, pure Stanislavski. The wish fathered the thought while necessity mothered invention, and I pressed buttons and flicked switches inside my head until I was what I seemed to be, an ignoble savage paying carnal homage to my white goddess. I lived the part and rose to the occasion, so to speak, and the lady was not displeased.

Her cries of passion would have been more inspiring had we not had a language in common. As she prepared to die the little death, she cried out in cadence and crescendo, and had I not understood the words I might have been moved. But what she cried out was the begat section of Genesis, singularly appropriate in a sense but hardly in line with my own mood.

We rested, and we resumed, and we rested once again. And then, while I lay with eyes lidded and chest heaving and mind wandering lonely as a cloud, I heard the voice of a child.

"Hello, Daddy. Hello, Mommy. May I go for a nice walk? May I play with my toys?"

I looked up to see who was addressing us as Daddy and Mommy. But there was no one in the room but me and the goddess, and I looked at her and away and back again in a rather clumsy double take. It was the goddess who was speaking, but in a distinctly ungoddessly voice.

"Mary had a little lamb," she began, in a tinny tiny voice, and went on, reciting this and other Mother Gooseries. She made occasional mistakes—she had trouble, for example, in keeping Little Boy Blue and Little Bo-peep straight, but then they may have had that problem themselves. The little voice never faltered and was never at a loss for words. I reached out, tipped up her chin, looked into her eyes. There was nobody home.

According to the script, it was just about time for me to put Sheena temporarily out of commission. The precise mechanics of this were to be improvised on the spot, and would probably involve something like bopping her over the head and tying her up.

I hadn't liked the idea then and I liked it less now. Some vestigial remnant of chivalry, anachronistic but undeniable for all that, made me less than enthusiastic about the prospect of treating any woman in this fashion. Women, after all, occupy a special niche in the great chain of being (if chains have niches). They stand (if one stands in niches) a little lower than the apes, a little higher than the angels. And they are to be approached courteously, and with respect, and not with a right to the jaw.

And if it is undecorous to knock a woman cold, it would seem just that much worse to do so after having shared a bed with her. I had taken this into consideration and had just about conquered my objections, and now yet another variable had been introduced. I had not merely shared a bed with Sheena. I had done so and had seen the bedding process induce a reversion to childhood. It was one thing to coldcock Sheena, Queen of the Jungle. It was another thing when Sheena had become Jane and when a child's voice emerged from that unimpeachably mature body.

"My name is Jane and I am ten years old. Are you a stranger? My mommy says I am not to talk to strangers. Are you a nice man? My name is Jane—"

She's a murderess, I told myself. A butcher. Next to her, Ilse Koch was just a life-of-the-party type with a lampshade on her head.

"My daddy is a man of God. He is tall and pretty. At night sometimes he sleeps with my mommy and they wrestle and call out God's name. I have to wash my hands and face and eat all my vegetables and say my prayers or I will not go to heaven when I die. When my daddy goes away my uncle Bobby goes with my mommy and they say their prayers and wrestle. My daddy's name is Mordecai. My mommy's name is Prudence. My name is Jane."

A cannibal, I thought. A butchering murdering cannibal. A menace.

"My name is Jane and I am ten years old—"

I swallowed. Whatever happened to Baby Jane, it had certainly left its mark on her. But underneath the animal skins and inside the lush flesh the innocent child lived on. It was all still there, trapped in a madwoman who roamed the jungle as if intent on having her life story serialized in the *National Enquirer.*

I said, "You poor little kid."

"My name is Jane. Who are you?"

"Evan."

"Jane, Evan. Evan, Jane."

"You poor screwed-up little kid."

"Round and round the mulberry bush to get a pail of water."

I went over to the front of the tent and peered out through the flap. The two sentries remained on duty. Beyond them, I saw the tournament in progress. Pairs of warriors faced one another and crouched, ready for combat. Sam Bowman called out a signal and two of them rushed each other, making sudden movements, thrusting, parrying. Then one straightened up and stood erect while the other lay still in the dust. The winner took his place in line, others carried the loser off to the side, and Bowman signaled another pair of combatants to center stage.

Behind me, Jane went on babbling in rhyme. I hissed a volley of sibilant syllables at the sentries. They turned, and I crooked a finger to motion one of them inside. He came, voicing some question or other. I turned and pointed wordlessly at Jane. He looked at her, and while he was thus occupied I hit him as one hits rabbits, with a fist to the back of the neck. It couldn't have worked very much better had he been a rabbit. He made a brief gurgling sound and then made no sound at all.

"Why did you hit the nice man, Evan? The black men are our friends. Daddy said we must be nice to the black men and teach them the word of the Lord. Uncle Bobby was a black man. Mommy taught Uncle Bobby the word of the Lord. Uncle Bobby was my friend. One day he showed me his—"

I hissed at the remaining sentry and went through the routine a second time. I pointed not at Jane but at the body of his fallen comrade, but with that exception it was an identical repeat performance. I was pretty good at hitting unsuspecting men in the back of the neck. Now I could try the same trick on Baby Jane Grey, and if I got high marks I could graduate to the next level, that of shooting fish in a barrel.

Why hit her? Why not just slip away and leave her? She was lost in childhood reverie, wrapped up in memories of what Uncle Bobby had shown her so long ago.

I went to her. She was reciting a poem, the words spilling from her lips in a childish singsong cadence. I found it as incomprehensible that I had recently bedded her as I did that she went around sacking missions and cutting people up. I said, "Jane," and put a hand on her shoulder.

Her eyes met mine, her beautiful empty eyes, and I watched as her eyes changed. Jane turned off and Sheena turned on, and her eyes probed mine, and she saw me as she had not seen me before. "White devil!" she shrilled, and leaped at me, hands out, fingers curled like hooks, nails flashing in the candlelight.

I hauled off and hit her in the head.

I found Plum at the river's edge. She was wrestling the long dugout canoes out into the water and sending them off downstream. This, we had determined, was the only way to render them *hors de combat*—chopping or burning through the thick sides and bottom would take forever, and they might float anyway. I gave Plum a hand, and we maneuvered them one at a time into the river and out of the picture.

"The first heat's over," I told her. "Half of the clowns have knocked the other half out. I got a close look at a couple of them, and I don't think they're pulling their punches. Some of the losers looked awfully dead."

"And now?"

"Now the winners pair off and do it again. When they've lowered the number of survivors to three or four, Bowman's going to finish them off himself. Of course they'll be the three or four best of the bunch, which might make it tough for him. That's the basic flaw."

"He told me that he welcomes the chance to match himself against the best of them. That he fears no man."

"Well, he's got an ego big as all outdoors. If his devotion to Knanda Ndoro's not an act, then the Retriever was the only man alive Bowman ever respected."

"You do not like him."

"Not too much, no." He had bugged me during the planning session, and I was still recovering from it. "But I have to admit that I'm glad he's on our side."

"We could leave now, Evan."

"Without him?"

She nodded. "We could take the last boat and just go. It would be easy for us. And he could get away by himself. I do not think he could catch us, not without a boat, and I do not think he would even try. Perhaps he would stay here with Sheena and her filthy killers. He was happy with them before. Perhaps it is the best life for him."

"I guess you aren't crazy about him, either."

"He always puts his hands on me. And makes remarks about my color. He is really enthusiastic about my color. Are there no girls of mixed blood in America?"

"There are thousands of them."

"Then why does he find me so exotic?"

"Consider it a tribute to your beauty."

"I do not wish such tributes. I have not told you this before, but you look ridiculous with your skin darkened. And with that horrid paint on yourself."

"You don't look so splendid, either."

"I do not feel splendid. Can we leave him, Evan? He causes me to feel dirty inside. Please?"

"No. No, we can't."

"I thought you would say that."

We managed to heave another canoe into the water and send it on its way. Plum wanted to know what happened with Sheena. I gave her an expurgated version. She was fascinated when I told her about the emergence of Baby Jane.

"She is how old, Evan? Ten? You see, it is even worse now than before. I am fourteen, and that is bad enough, but now you have made love with a ten-year-old."

"Cut it out."

"You must be ashamed of yourself."

"Dammit, Plum—"

"But perhaps it is all right because you are married

to her, Evan." She giggled merrily. "Now you must not make love to me any more. I am not the sort who would have relations with a married man."

"That's fine with me."

She tossed her head. "I will have to content myself with Sam."

"You stay away from—"

"Oh? You are suddenly jealous?"

"I'm not jealous."

"You have only my best interests at heart."

"Right the first time."

"Perhaps I could consider adultery after all—"

All but one of the boats was afloat now. I pulled myself up onto the bank and shook off the excess water. "Some other time," I told her. "You wait here. I have to see how Bowman's coming along."

"It would be easy to leave now, Evan. Without him."

"I know," I said, and headed back to camp.

Bowman was beautiful to watch. I found someone's abandoned machete and sat in the shadows with it, waiting for him to need help. He never did. He just kept hanging in there, letting the troops decrease from fifty to twenty-five to thirteen to seven to four, and while two men were joined in brief combat he worked his way around among the fallen. Whenever one of them threatened to regain consciousness, he would wait until all eyes were riveted on the combatants before moving to apply a kick or chop to some vital center. When the four were narrowed down to two, he stood them next to one another, stepped alongside of them, and knocked their heads together. I had heard of knocking two clowns' heads together often enough, but this was the first time I had actually seen anyone do it. After such a display of advanced judo technique there was something shocking about such a primitive act as this. But you couldn't fault it for effectiveness. There was a marvelous clunking sound and that was it. They fell, and stayed put.

He had his back to me when he finished. I stood up and took a step forward, and he spun around to face me, moving at the speed, I would guess, of light. I was holding onto the machete, but I realized instinctively that the sight of it would not stop him from flinging himself at me, nor would the use of it do much more than slow him down a fraction. I shouted out that I was me, and his hands dropped to his sides even as his face relaxed in the now-familiar grin.

He said, "Shee-it, Tanner cat, you has missed all the fun. Or were you around for the finale?"

"I caught the last act."

"Like cracking coconuts. I told you there'd be nothing to it. Once you get people trustin' you, ain't a whole lot you can't get by with."

"True enough."

"You make out good with the Queen of the Jungle?"

"Something strange happened."

"Lady Jane?"

"Oh. She's made that trip before?"

"Every time, man. Sends me up the wall."

"You might have told me."

"And ruin the surprise?" He slapped me on the back,

which was something I would have just as soon he hadn't bothered doing. "I just figured you might like findin' out about it all by yourself. First time she tried that on I went bonkers, baby. I bet you heard all about Mommy and Daddy and Uncle Bobby."

"I bet I did."

"Lady Jane came by that taste for dark meat honest-like. Inherited it from her old lady. You put her out?"

"Yes."

"Kill her?"

"Of course not."

"Just that I was thinkin' you maybe should. She plays mean, you know. The way she gets on with these bush types, she'll have fifty fresh men in colors by daybreak. I wouldn't want to meet up with her again."

"Just kill her," I said.

"Easiest way."

"Just like that."

He clapped me on the shoulder again. Plum had a point, I thought; he would be a real pleasure to abandon. He said, "You gettin' butterflies, Tanner cat. I'll go on and do it for you. Don't make me no never mind."

"No."

"If you want."

"No," I said. "No, go down by the river, give Plum a hand." An unfortunate choice of words, that. "I'll be along."

I was panting by the time I reached the riverbank. I got to where the boat was beached and my knees started to buckle, but I stayed on my feet.

Plum and Sam were looking at me as though I had lost my mind.

"Tanner cat—"

"Evan—"

"Not now," I said. "I can't talk. I can barely breathe. Later."

"But—"

"Later."

I put Sheena in the back of the dugout and arranged her animal skins over her. Then I straightened up again and tried to catch my breath.

Bowman was scratching his head. Plum was shaking hers. I couldn't honestly blame them, but I was damned if I felt like talking about it.

Chapter 13

Some conversations which took place between or among various persons floating down the Yellowfoot River over a period of several days:

"Tanner cat, you must be out of your head. Like totally stone bonkers."

"Ours not to reason why."

"How's that, man?"

"You know the Chief, Bowman cat. You worked for him long enough yourself. When he gives out an assignment, he wants it followed every step of the way. Right?"

"Right as rain. But—"

"The last thing he wants to see is a man who starts improvising. He wants me to carry out the plan. I could try to simplify things, and if I was all alone I might. But I've got you along for the ride, and that makes it different."

"How so?"

"He might hear from you that I left Sheena to go on queening it."

"You think I'd tell him?"

"I don't even trust myself, Bowman cat."

"A sound policy. You never said Sheena was part of the assignment."

"You never asked."

"Yeah, well. What's so important about her?"

"That's just one of the things the Chief keeps under that crazy plaid hat he always wears."

"That nutty old hat."

"You know it, man. I don't ask him embarrassing questions. I just follow orders. Saves a lot of heartache when it's time to type up the report."

"Evan? Obviously you no longer love me. You love this white woman."

"There's a big difference between love and the milk of human kindness."

"Would you overflow with this milk if she were not beautiful?"

"Oh, don't be silly, Plum."

"It is enough that we are encumbered with him. My bottom is sore from pinches. I do not think I can endure very much more of this, Evan."

"I thought he was keeping hands off."

"Well, he is not. I believe it was a mistake to take the stain out of my hair and skin. I believe it is my color that has this effect upon him. Evan?"

"What?"

"Can we not put her overboard?"

"Plum, you're being very foolish about this. She was a ten-year-old girl, a child. And that personality is all locked up inside her just waiting to be brought to the surface."

"I have not seen it. When she is awake she does nothing but call down the wrath of the Lord upon us."

"She's being Sheena now. When she's Jane—"

"I have never seen her be Jane."

"Well, she only does it after an experience that moves her very deeply."

"I believe I know the sort of experience you mean."

"I thought you might."

"Is that what you plan, Evan? You will give her such experiences constantly so that she will remain Jane?"

"Oh, cut it out, will you? Look, there are clinics that can do wonders with personality disorders like this. It's just a matter of rooting out the Sheena person and bringing the Jane person to the surface."

"And then there will be this beautiful woman with the mind of a ten-year-old."

"Well, most beautiful women have the mind of a ten-year-old."

"Evan—"

"Some other time, okay? I think he's waking up."

"No, he sleeps. Evan, I was—"

"You're not paddling right, Plum. Try to slip your blade into the water at a little more of an angle."

"Like this?"

"That's a little better."

"But that is how I was doing it. I believe you are attempting to change the subject, Evan."

"Why, that's very perceptive of you, Plum."

"Opium."

"That's what it is, Tanner cat. Fields and fields of it. As far as the eye can see. Nothing but instant happiness growing up nice and green."

"Miles of opium. I suppose you could call it a growing monument to the Modonoland Retriever."

"It's his monument is what it is. Before he thought to plant it, this country didn't have a thing going for it. Tons of potential but not a pound of right-now action, you dig? Wasn't nothin' Modonoland could produce that somebody else couldn't manage cheaper and faster and better. But when you come to opium you've got a seller's market. And ain't nobody else on the continent that's growin' it."

"There's the little matter of international law."

"International laws are made to be broken, man. Nobody pays any attention to them if they cut you out of a dollar. Look, who makes the money out of opium if Modonoland don't? Nobody but China."

"That's one way to look at it."

"What's good for Modonoland—"

"Uh-huh. I understand the Glorious Retriever made a few cents himself from the opium."

"That's the American Way, ain't it?"

"Don't be touchy."

"Ain't bein' touchy, man. Only—"

"My point was that the royal treasure must have come to quite a sum."

"It must have done, I suppose."

"I wonder what happened to the treasure."

"Still back in Griggstown, I reckon."

"I don't."

"That right?"

"Uh-huh. We know Knanda Ndoro got it out. A fortune in negotiable paper and cut gems, according to what we heard."

"You heard that."

"Uh-huh. I thought you might be carrying it, but you didn't bring it on the boat. Where is it stashed?"

"The Retriever hid it."

"And died without being able to tell you where he had put it?"

"I don't know as you'll buy that one."

"Not much chance that I will."

"Well, then."

"Be tough for you to get it out of the country on your own, Bowman cat. But I've got worlds of contacts. MMM people and such."

"You know those creeps?"

"Uh-huh. They might be handy."

"Might. Course, a straight arrow like you, Tanner cat, like you would want to turn it all over to the man with the plaid hat."

"I might not be all that straight myself, Bowman cat."

"That so?"

"That's so."

"I might maybe like to think on that a spell."

"You might at that."

"Hey, Plum kitten."

"No."

"Now you are being silly."

"Stay where you are. You will tip the boat."

"Couldn't tip this battleship with twenty men. What I want to know is why old Tanner cat has to always sleep in the middle. Like he's trying to keep us two apart."

"Look, I don't—"

"No sense in you bein' all hung up on him. He don't care for you."

"How do you know?"

"What he said."

"You're lying."

"And the way he's actin'. Why you think he brought old Sheena girl along? You never heard him say nothin' about bringin' her until he put it to her, did you? But soon as he had it off with her, then he's keen on bringin' her along. He's just not your kind, kitten, and you ain't his kind, and she is."

"Or your kind either."

"Oh, now. Close enough."

"And I'm only a child. I don't suppose that means anything to you, does it?"

"You big enough, you old enough."

"Go away. Please! Anyway, I think Evan is waking up."

"He's sleepin'."

"I think he's waking up."

"Say, I thought on what you said, man."

"Oh."

"About that treasure and all."

"And?"

"I could give you half."

"That sounds generous."

"Well, we's in this together, right? Share and share alike. I give you too little and I got a discontented cat on my hands, and one thing I don't want is a discontented cat on my hands."

"Where's the treasure?"

"Well, see, it never did get out of Griggstown."

"I thought that—"

"No, see, what happened was we got it out of the palace, and then we was supposed to get a ship out of there, but the ship wasn't in the right place at the right time. So we stashed the goodies in the shipyard."

"In the shipyard."

"I could tell you just where, but I might could make a mistake. I tend to disremember precise details like that."

"I'll bet you do."

"Right up close, now, I would remember that sort of thing. But now I ain't too clear on it."

"I can understand that."

"Yeah. Very heavy, don't you think?"

"Heavy. Speaking of which, you're coming on too heavy with Plum."

"Oh?"

"Yeah. It might be nice if you cooled it a little."

"You never said you objected."

"*She* objected."

"Well, she ain't but a girl, baby. I knew you were havin' it off with her but I never thought you figured you had an exclusive. All you had to do was say."

"Then I'm saying."

"Because I didn't think you been doin' anythin' with her since we got on this here hollow log of a boat, and I thought if you didn't then—"

"Well, now you know different, don't you?"

"I surely do. And since we're buddies, I wouldn't think to cut in while you're dancin'."

"That's what I thought. Besides, you wouldn't really want Plum anyway. You know she's half white."

"That's a fact."

"As soon as we get back home, you can get yourself a beautiful black woman in Bed-Stuy."

"Now you talkin'. Soon as I get back home to Oakland, that's what I'm gonna get, a beautiful black woman in bed."

Just some conversations which took place between or among various persons floating down the Yellowfoot River over a period of several days.

Chapter 14

Fortunately it was not all talk. Otherwise we would have gone mad. But the conversations were separated by long silences, long lazy hours of lackadaisical paddling down the broad meandering sleepy old Yellowfoot. The river wandered all over the place, and we spent as much time shifting from left to right and back again as we did making real progress toward the capital. We sat, the four of us, in the hollowed-out trunk of a wali tree, and we floated and paddled first through the overgrown jungle land and then through the flat coastal plain where the opium grew. We caught fish in the river. We picked fruit and dug roots and pulled up greens on the banks. It was not a diet to grow fat on, but neither was it as troubling to the mind as Stew à la Sheena.

The weather was good, the heat not too deadening, the rain light and infrequent. The local fauna did a good job of leaving us alone. Crocodiles floated at the water's surface or sunned themselves upon the muddy banks. They bobbed in the soupy water like logs, and perhaps they took our dugout for the grandfather of all crocodiles; at any rate they left us quite alone. Mosquitoes were either not abundant or not hungry. No flies swarmed at us.

There was, in fact, that special feeling of sublime peace that could only be the calm before the storm. We spoke no harsh words to each other, we were quite considerate of one another, and yet this was by no means the result of bonds of good feeling uniting us in peace and fellowship.

More than once, as I feigned sleep, did I sense that Bowman was considering feeding me to the crocodiles. More than once did I detect in Plum's expression a desire to pack the Queen of the Jungle off to the Happy Hunting Grounds. And, in a less murderous vein, each of us was upset about something or other. I was irritated with Plum because she was behaving childishly. She was annoyed with me because I wasn't behaving loverishly, and because she blamed me for the unwelcome presence of the other two. I trusted Bowman about as far as I could throw him, and he didn't trust me nearly as far as he could throw me. He hated Plum because she wouldn't let him and she hated him because he wouldn't stop trying.

Sheena, my wife, hated all of us but had to keep it to herself. We kept her trussed up in the rear of the dugout and kept a rag stuffed in her mouth except at feeding time. It seems excessive in retrospect, two presumably grown men keeping a girl tied and gagged, but she was wholly uncontrollable otherwise, much given to ear bursting wails and oaths and quite determined to turn the boat over and drown us all. Her strength was as the strength of ten, not because her heart was pure, God knows, but because she fought with the single-minded determination of the truly flipped-out. Inside there, I kept telling myself, was an innocent little girl. But there were times when I, too, would have loved to let her go for a terminal swim.

That, then, was the sort of special peace of the voyage. A lazy peaceful time during which I would pretend to go to sleep in the middle of our little boat, with my hand always clenched on the hilt of my machete. A lazy peaceful time given to thoughts of Kitty, my wife to be, and Sheena, whom I had recently agreed to take for better or for worse. (Hardly a legal ceremony in anyone's eyes, and yet if a ship's captain could perform marriages on the high seas, couldn't a cannibal queen in her camp?) I thought about Plum, and I thought about Samuel Lonestar Bowman, and I thought about the undying specter of Knanda Ndoro, the Glorious Retriever of Modonoland. What, I wondered, did a Modonoland Retriever do? A Labrador Retriever was obviously something that retrieved Labradors, but—

One night, just as the sun was dropping out of sight, Bowman turned poet again. He got carried away with the placid flow of the river and the lush beauty of the countryside and the sound of his own voice. How beautiful it was, he said, and how peaceful.

"It is utterly perfect," Plum said, her lip curling. "It is truly a shame that our voyage must come to an end."

More of a shame than she thought. Any sort of calm period is to be treasured for its own sake, I think, without regard to the conflict that must inevitably end it. On either a personal or a global scale, peace is that stretch of time during which preparations are made for the next war. This doesn't make it any less satisfying.

Admittedly, though, the maintenance of this particular peace required a special sort of brinkmanship. In a sense our dugout was a Cold War world in microcosm, with an added similarity in that it was impossible to be sure just who was on who's side, or just what the fighting was about. The true test of skill came when we ran the boat up on the bank and one or more of us got busy gathering brush for a cookfire, or pulling up edible weeds in the opium fields, or performing such bodily functions as are best performed in private. The object was to avoid leaving a fatal combination of persons together. If Plum and Bowman remained unattended, for example, he might ravish her. If Plum had unsupervised custody of Sheena, she might do something antisocial.

It wasn't really quite that spooky, but it seemed that way now and again. It was, as I once remarked to Plum, like the old brain twister about the cannibals and the missionaries. Plum chose to miss the point. "There is only one cannibal," she said icily.

"Technically you might say we're all cannibals."

"I had none of that stew, Evan."

"Let's talk about something else."

We talked of other things, and of nothing at all, and one day followed another as days are wont to do, and the river, for all its shilly-shallying, flowed indefatigably to the sea, as rivers are wont to do.

Early in the morning of what ultimately proved to be a Thursday, we hit the outlying districts of the capital. By daybreak we were securely lodged in a neat little suburban house not unlike the one from which I had liberated the Volkswagen back when all of this was just getting started. We had walked through those dark and empty streets, and I quickly selected an empty house. Nothing could have been simpler. I merely looked for a house with a couple of lights on. People who go out of town always leave a light on, so that a burglar won't drive by in the early evening and see their house just sitting there, dark and vacant. But should the same burglar drive by at, say, four in the morning, he would see their house more conspicuous than ever, light and vacant. Had we gotten to town in the early evening, this house certainly would have fooled us. We didn't, and it didn't, and a further check showed that the car was not in the garage, and a still further check revealed a note in the milk box—"Milkman/Please No Milk Until a Week from Monday Because We Are Going Away/ Mrs. Penner." I experimented with various blades of the Swiss Army pocketknife, trying to find one that would slip between door and frame and snick the bolt back. The screwdriver seemed the most likely choice, but it wasn't working.

Bowman said, "Let me try, Tanner cat." I turned to hand him the knife but he ignored it and eased me out of the way. He hit the glass panel at the side of the door. It shattered, and he reached inside and turned the knob, and the door opened.

I said, "Oh."

"Saves time."

The Penners had a beautiful stainless-steel and formica kitchen stocked with every conceivable labor-saving device, so many of them that one could spend several hours a day flicking switches and pressing buttons. All of the major appliances were powder blue, and the walls and ceiling of the cute little kitchen were a complementary shade of blue, and the whole thing was really lovely. The best part of all was the inside of the refrigerator. It was full.

Bowman carried Sheena into one of the bedrooms and tucked her in, piling her animal skins on top of her. Plum collected items of clothing from us and went into the utility room, where she put them through the washing machine. I stayed in that gorgeous spotless kitchen and made a pot of coffee and began cooking things.

We ate, drank coffee, ate more, drank more coffee. I took a plate of food to Sheena, untied her, fed her, tied her up again. She was terrible company but there was really nothing to be done about it; the Jane personality could only be brought to the surface through a singular form of shock treatment. I went back to the kitchen. Plum reported that our clothes had largely fallen apart in the washing machine. We were wearing various articles which the Penners had evidently not needed on their vacation—a horrible plaid beach robe for me, a rainbow-hued nylon duster for Plum, a belted trench coat for Sam. The duster was about the right size, but Mr. Penner was a distinctly small man. His robe was tight on me, and his trench coat was absurd on Bowman, who had trouble moving his arms. These would do for the time being, we decided. Soon we would all be going to sleep, anyway. And at night Plum could put on something of Mrs. Penner's, something that would do while she scooted over to a friend's house and foraged suitable clothing for all of us, and whatever other assistance we might require.

"The thing is," Bowman said, "that we all ought to get to sleep soon as we can."

"Actually," I said, "I'm not all that tired."

"Man, you been goin' for the longest time. You better get some sleep for yourself."

"Evan hardly sleeps at all," Plum said.

"Just buildin' up for a real breakdown, that's all you're doin', man."

But I was a real pain in the neck. I just didn't feel like going to sleep, and I seemed determined to keep everyone awake while forcing cup after cup of bad coffee into all of us. I was bursting with plans, plans for recovering the treasure, plans for getting out of Modonoland undiscovered. No one else seemed even vaguely interested in discussing these plans, or indeed in discussing anything at all. Bowman appeared distinctly irritated, while Plum merely looked exhausted. I was oblivious to all of this. Coffeepot in one hand and machete in the other—I just always seemed to have that machete in my hand, strangely enough—I led the way into the family room and switched on the radio.

"A family room," I said. "A radio, a color television set, a record player, a tape recorder—this is great, isn't it? I'll have to have all of these things when I have my house in the suburbs. All the latest things, all the conveniences." I was babbling. "An electric wall-to-wall carpet. An automatic spoon. An electric blackboard in living color."

"It sounds very Donald Duck," Plum said.

Bowman said, "Donald Duck?"

"She means Mickey Mouse," I explained. He seemed no less mystified than before, and no more interested. He suggested that I was out on my feet and that we ought to get to sleep.

I had stalled as long as I could. The radio had yielded nothing in the way of news, just some unnecessary music. I switched it off. Plum went to share a twin-bed room with Sheena. She wasn't happy about it, but was too tired to protest much. The cumulative exhaustion of all those nights without one real night's sleep hit her all at once, and she slipped out of the wrapper and under the top sheet and fell asleep before the sheet had settled into place about her.

There was another bedroom with a cot in it, and there was a somewhat forbidding couch in the family room. I told Bowman I would take it. He did not agree.

"Not a chance, baby. You been livin' on nerves since we connected. I can see how tired you are. Your eyes are heavy, heavy." His eyes gleamed hypnotically. "You need sleep."

"But you're too big for the couch."

"I'm too long for the bed is what I am. I get uncomfortable in them little cots. On a couch, now, I can put my feet up on the armrest and be right comfortable."

"If you're sure."

"I'm sure."

I went into the bedroom and closed the door. I stretched out on the bed and waited. He was right. I had been living on nerves for far too long, and I was tired, and my eyes were heavy, heavy.

I had trouble staying in that room. A couple of times I wanted to go in and check, but didn't. Then I heard the couch creak as he got up from it, and I heard his steps on the floor of the family room. I had unplugged the bedside lamp earlier and wrapped the cord around the base, and now I grabbed it up and stood to the side of the door, ready to take him the minute he gave me a clear shot. I was going to have one shot and one shot only, and if I didn't get him the first try I could kiss my ass good-by. I had seen him in action. I knew.

The footsteps approached, stopped. There was a long moment of silence. Then his hand settled on the knob, and I saw the knob on my side of the door move slightly.

He spoke my name once, waited, said it again louder. I didn't say anything. The doorknob turned. The door opened slowly, very slowly, and his head came through, and my hand tightened on the lamp as I readied myself for the blow.

He took one step inside, his eyes peering at my bed, and I was ready to strike when his jaw worked spasmodically and he started down. I never touched him. He fell like a tree, fell in one stiff-legged motion, fell neatly forward and smacked his head on the floor.

He slept for ten hours. He came to late in the afternoon. I was sitting by the side of the bed when consciousness returned. He tensed his muscles and strained, and veins stood out on his temples and forehead and a pulse worked in his throat. I thought for a moment that he would burst his bonds. I had tied him up securely with half a dozen electrical cords and Mrs. Penner's fifty feet of clothesline, and even so I wasn't sure it would hold him. The sonofabitch was unbelievably strong.

He went limp again, his eyes opened, and he saw me. He became extremely scrutable. A full complement of emotions played over his handsome face.

He said, "You were ready for me."

"I was."

"You weren't asleep."

"I wasn't."

"You hit me with something."

"Never touched you."

"I feel like I been drugged."

"That's what happened, all right."

"With what?"

"Opium."

The eyes widened. "How?"

"In your coffee. I gathered a little of it every time I wandered into the fields."

"And here I thought you had dysentery, Tanner cat."

"It was harvest time on the old plantation," I went on. "Did you ever see how they gather opium? A week or so after the petals drop they cut into the fruit. Then they let it go on ripening, and the good stuff drains out of the opium fruit and hardens. Then they go through again and collect it."

"And you put it in my coffee."

"Uh-huh."

"How'd you know how much to use?"

"I didn't. I wasn't worried about using too much.

After all, it was completely raw opium. Not refined into morphine or codeine or anything. The only thing I was worried about was that you would taste it in the coffee."

"That was pretty horrible tasting coffee, all right."

"I didn't think it would have as much effect as it did. It probably wouldn't have if you hadn't been close to the edge of exhaustion to begin with. Even so, you held out for a long time before it knocked you down. I was just hoping it would take the edge off your reflexes, even things out a little."

He thought this over. "Well, Tanner cat," he said at length, "I reckon I can see where it all lays. You want to do me out of my half of the Retriever's treasury. And you also want to make sure I don't inform on you to the Old Man. I can see your point, but the thing is—"

"Wrong."

"Huh?"

"The Chief never wore a hat in his life. Bed-Stuy is a part of Brooklyn. And you ain't Bowman cat, Bowman cat. You're the Glorious Retriever of Modonoland, and do I call you Knanda or Ndoro or both?"

Chapter 15

After a few moments of respectful silence he said, "I am rather glad to have that out of the way, Tanner. Actually I was surprised the deception succeeded as long as it did. It was a difficult role to play." His manner was entirely different now, the voice rich and resonant, the tones properly pear-shaped. He sounded like the announcer on the old *Shadow* radio program—*Who knows what evil lurks in the hearts of men?*

I said, "The Shadow do."

"Pardon me?"

"An old joke."

"Quite. I was saying that the role was not an easy one for me. Bowman was a crude, rough type. There was a raw primitive quality about him that was not without appeal, however. I doubt I'd have thought to pose as him if you hadn't virtually put the suggestion into my head by greeting me with his name.

"You recognized the agency recognition signal."

"Ah, yes. It was one of the items the man disclosed to me. Not the only one." He smiled a private smile, a sly smile, not the easy grin he had used during the masquerade. "I must say I enjoyed playing the part. And it did take you in for rather a long time."

"Not really."

"Oh?"

I told him I'd known for a long time. That there was too much happening in his colloquialisms, too many outdated phrases mixed in with newer expressions. "And too many Britishisms. Not just the odd items Bowman might have picked up through exposure to you, not just bits he might have affected, but turns of phrase that would only be possible to someone whose education was British rather than American."

"And I had fancied myself equipped with a keen ear for just that."

"Oh, you're good at it. You sound right most of the time. But it's one thing to know how to use the regionalisms of another area and another to keep your own regionalisms out of your talk."

"Quite."

"And there were other things, too. The absolute fascination with Plum."

"A fascinating girl. And Bowman did like women, you know."

"But he wouldn't be struck by the idea of a mixed-blood girl. Plum's color really got to you. It's a nice enough color, but it's not as rare as you made it seem. Not in America, certainly. Some of the stanchest black nationalists are as light-skinned as Plum is. But that kind of racial mixture is rare in Modonoland."

"I never considered that."

"It didn't surprise Plum. She's used to being considered exotic and unusual. But in America—"

He nodded. "And of course I was completely at sea

when we discussed your chief and his manner of opera-
tion. I almost suspected that might be a test but I could
only play it by ear." He frowned. "You say you knew
for some time."

"Yes."

"That I was not Bowman? Or that I was Knanda
Ndoro?"

"Both, really. The clincher was your story about how
the Retriever died."

"I thought it was a touching speech."

"Oh, it was."

"But Bowman wouldn't have been capable of such
bathos? Perhaps not."

"Probably not," I agreed. "But I didn't know anything much about Bowman. No, the thing was that *you*
couldn't be capable of that much respect for anyone but
yourself. Everything about you was one big ego trip. I
got the message intuitively, but thinking about it just
reinforced it. You had to be Knanda Ndoro; the only
real hero in your eyes is you yourself."

"That's interesting," he said. "That's very interesting." He frowned for a few moments, thinking it over.
Then he grunted with annoyance. "You know," he said,
"this is bloody awkward. This business of being trussed
up like a goat awaiting a barbecue. Don't you think you
might cut me loose so we can discuss this sensibly as
equals?"

"No."

"A flat no?"

"A flat no."

The grin came suddenly, rich and easy. In his Bowman voice he said, "Well, Tanner cat, you can't put me down for trying it on."

"That's an example." He looked puzzled. "*Trying it on.* Bowman wouldn't have said that."

He filed this bit of information away. I could almost see it being shuttled off to the proper mental pigeonhole. We talked some more about Americanisms and Britishisms and a few Africanisms, and about his eulogy for his own self.

"Every tragic hero has a single abiding flaw," he mused. "I fear mine is a lack of humility. I don't think I ever saw any point in humility. From boyhood it never occurred to me that I had anything to be humble about. My own basic superiority was always patently obvious to me, and I assumed it must be equally obvious to others, or that it would be, had they the sense to see it."

"What happened to Bowman?"

"Bowman? He died of the fever I invented for myself. I buried him. Not by clawing the dirt away with my hands, I'm afraid, and without benefit of Stevensonian epitaphs, but otherwise it was much as I said it."

"I see."

He started to say something, paused, then changed direction. "If you've known for so long that I am who I am, why go along with the deception?"

"I didn't want to die of a fever."

"Pardon?"

"I think you would have killed us if you knew we knew."

"Why would I do that?"

"I don't know. Why did you kill Bowman?"

"I told you—"

"Don't bother."

"Hmmm," he said. Suddenly he laughed, a rich warm vibrant laugh that in context I found quite chilling. "Bowman wanted my wealth. Mine! And he wanted it. He had a suitcase full of ideas, Bowman did. He would take me back to America. My bearer bonds and certificates of deposit and my gems, these would finance a black revolution in America. We would split off a dozen southern states, he told me, and we would establish a black government there."

"He wasn't the first man with that dream."

"Perhaps not. That made it no more attractive to me. If you're as sound a man as you seem, Tanner, you know that a black government in America has as much chance for success as a white government in Africa. This one, for example—these white men will all be hanging from lampposts one of these days. And so would Bowman if he took his ideas back to America. I had no desire to invest my funds in such an enterprise. Nor was I by any means certain that Bowman wanted only a portion of the fortune, or that he intended to take me back to America along with my money. I had the distinct impression, friend Tanner, that it was a simple matter of survival. One or the other of us was going to die of a jungle fever. And while I was better than he at hand-to-hand techniques, that was no guarantee that he might not—uh, induce a fever, shall we say, when my back was turned. I had to act first."

"And you had to act first here, too. With me."

"An unpleasant subject, that."

"As unpleasant for me as it is for you."

"Of course I wouldn't have killed you," he said.

"Of course not."

"I just would have discommoded you temporarily while I made my escape."

"I'm sure of it."

He laughed suddenly, like a seal barking. "Oh, Tanner," he said. "It's a pleasure to have everything out in the open, isn't it?"

"Is it?"

"Unquestionably. We're at rather a stalemate, aren't we, though? I don't suppose either of us is entirely willing to put much trust in the other, and yet we have to do precisely that, don't we?"

"Why?"

"Because we need each other."

"For what?"

His eyes flashed but his voice remained cool, confident, on top of it all. "Nothing's really changed," he said. "You need me to get a portion of the treasure. You don't know where it is and there's no way you can find it on your own. You can search the shipyard until the tide goes out permanently. It won't do you any good."

"I see."

"I'm sure you do." He beamed. "You have me all wrapped up like a parcel, but I'm really on an equal footing, am I not?" His deep voice echoed in the room. "You'll get no information from me, Tanner. I'm not easily intimidated. Pain does not move me, threats do not bother me. We will work this all out my way."

"And what's that?"

"You will untie me. Now. And you and your little brown girl will wait here while I recover the fortune myself. Then I will return—"

"Sure you will."

"Why, I still need your help to get out of the country. I could do it without you, but why should I? You already know everything. And we really do need each other, Tanner. With your help I might get into the United States. I suspect I might find your country a good home for my talents. The market for African leaders is crowded now, you know. As a superior African of some wealth, I could have a secure future in America."

"So you would come back on your own, and then the four of us would waltz off together."

"Precisely."

"And we would split the fortune according to plan, and we would all be satisfied."

"There is enough for all."

"Uh-huh."

"So it is settled. Now if you will cut these bonds—"

"But nothing's settled," I said. "I may be crazy but I'm not stupid. Not that stupid, anyway. Even if what you said made perfect sense, I don't believe you'd stick with it. Your ego wouldn't let you be equal partners with anyone in anything."

His face hardened. "You will never get the treasure without my help."

"I know."

"And you cannot possibly get my help except on my terms."

"I know."

He frowned. "Then what will you do?"

"I will get the hell out of this godforsaken country," I said. "Your treasure can stay here, and so can you. I don't really care about your fortune. I didn't come here to get rich, and I don't really have any use for the money now. I have to get back home and buy a house something like this one, except maybe a little bigger, and without quite so much plastic in it. And then I have to marry a girl named Katin Bazerian and adopt the heir apparent to the throne of Lithuania. Heiress apparent, that is. And then I have to live happily ever after, and I can do that without your bearer bonds and your diamonds and whatever the hell else you've got. And without your monumental ego for company, for that matter."

"You will just . . . just leave?"

"That's the idea."

"And the fortune? You will leave it for me?"

"Right."

"Well," he said. "That is—"

"But you probably won't get much pleasure out of it. Because I'll leave you here, tied up like this, so that you won't spoil our exit. And I'll leave Sheena here, too, because I don't see how I could get her out of here under the circumstances, and because you'll need someone to keep you company. And I guess I'll leave her untied, because otherwise she might starve to death, and I wouldn't want that on my conscience."

He was staring at me.

"And whether she'll have any particular animosity

toward the man who sold her down the river, and I do mean down the river, well, I wouldn't know about that. You'll just have to see."

I got up and started for the door.

"Wait," he said. "Wait. We must talk this over."

Chapter 16

A journey of a thousand miles begins with a single step, or so they tell me. It occurred to me now that a journey of not too much less than a thousand miles could have been avoided if I had taken a few dozen well-chosen steps at the onset. For we had indeed come full circle, and the final act of our little drama was being staged in the very cemetery where it all began, and not fifty yards from the grave where I had been buried alive.

The moon beamed benevolently down upon us, and the stars contributed their conspiratorial winks. Plum, gaily outfitted in Mrs. Penner's lime green bermuda shorts and burnt orange sleeveless blouse, reinforced this illumination with Mr. Penner's flashlight. I still had the machete which had belonged to some poor cannibal, and to some rather less fortunate mission field hand before him. It hung from my belt—Mr. Penner's belt, that is, made suitable for me with a fresh hole courtesy of the belt-hole blade of the Swiss Army pocketknife. And in my hands I held Mr. Penner's over-and-under shotgun, a weapon in which I had more faith than I vested in the machete and the Swiss Army pocketknife combined.

Both the flashlight and the shotgun were very sincerely pointed at Knanda Ndoro. He, too, wore some clothing of Mr. Penner's—a pair of bathing trunks and a pair of beach sandals and nothing else. And he, too, held an implement of Mr. Penner's—a garden shovel, with which he was opening a grave.

It was, I felt, an ideal division of labor. Plum, abetted by moon and stars, supplied the light. I served as the security force. And Knanda Ndoro did the retrieving.

The hole was about three feet deep when he heaved a sigh and leaned on his shovel as if our expedition were a WPA project. "This hardly seems equitable," he said. "I'm still groggy from that bloody opium, you know. And here you have me doing nigger work. You've the soul of a colonialist exploiter, Tanner."

"Did you make Sam Bowman do his own digging?"

"There was no digging to do. The grave was open. The gravediggers are an odd lot. They seem to work when the spirit moves them. They'd buried some poor bugger, dropped the casket in the hole without shoveling on the lid. I put the treasure in and filled the hole for them."

"With Sam Bowman in it."

"There was room."

Plum trembled involuntarily, and the flashlight beam danced. "You can't make him sound like a martyr," Knanda Ndoro went on, chatting pleasantly. "He was no angel, you know. I don't think you would have liked him at all."

"Dig."

He hefted the shovel, sent the blade biting into the

rich black soil. His skin, glossy with perspiration, gleamed in the flashlight's beam. He wielded the shovel with little visible effort, his muscles rippling beneath the smooth skin, the pile of dirt growing at the side of the hole.

"A schemer," he said, talking as he worked. "A plotter, a criminal, and a compulsive babbler. I've been an *aficionado* of Harlem culture for years, Tanner, but your man Bowman told me rather more about it than I cared to hear. I soaked it all up almost in spite of myself. I believe I gave a rather good verbal imitation of him. I may have made mistakes, but you must admit I had the accent right."

"Mmm," I said agreeably.

"But then I'm an adaptable sort. I've often reflected that this is a test of greatness, the capacity to adjust to adverse conditions and make the best of them. After I was forced to put an end to Bowman, for example, I had to make fresh plans for escaping from the country. I did so. They fell through, a dreadful example of things going wrong. I barely escaped with my life. Without hesitation I headed for the interior. I've lived in urban centers all my life, and yet I adapted to the countryside, learned to live off it. When I encountered that white girl and her little band of madmen I didn't give up and die. Nor did I try to flee. Instead I took command. Some men are born to lead, Tanner, and others are born to follow. True leaders have presence. Even those pitiful savages recognized this, just as they responded to the force of the white girl's persona. I drilled them into my own private army. I learned their ridiculous dialect. I won their trust. In time I might have used them a stepping-stone back to power. At least I toyed with the idea for lack of anything better.

"Then you turned up, and again I grasped the essence of the situation and looked for a better way. By using you and the child I could return to Griggstown, get clear of the savages. By letting you think I was Bowman I could take advantage of your help." The disarming smile. "I can scarcely pretend that everything's gone completely according to plan. One can never prepare for every possible contingency. And I do have that one flaw of insufficient humility against which I shall have to guard in the future."

"I sincerely hope so."

"You needn't worry." The shovel sank into the earth, the muscles worked, and another load of dirt was transferred from the hole to the pile. "Not everything has gone according to plan," he went on. "But everything's worked well enough."

"Then why are you the one with the shovel?"

"That's a small point, isn't it? We'll all come out of this well enough."

The flashing smile again, and I thought that it was literally disarming—it had the effect of unloading the shotgun even as I clutched it. The man's presence and force of personality were extraordinary. I had the gun and he had the shovel, but his manner stripped us both of these tools and made us equal partners in an enterprise.

He fell silent, and the pile of earth grew as the hole deepened. Plum held onto the flashlight and I held onto the shotgun. The shovel sank into the pit, and the Glorious Retriever sighed with satisfaction.

"Soon," he said. "I believe I've hit it."

"The treasure?"

He shook his head. "That's in a metal case. It would make another sort of noise entirely. I think I've hit the body."

He dug some more, and it seemed that he was right. The aroma of carrion filled the air. Then the shovel did hit something metallic, and he used the shovel to scrape off dirt. He set the shovel aside, lifted a huge metal lockbox out of the pit, and climbed out after it.

"Now," he said, setting the box down. "Now we'll just—God in heaven!"

He started at the yawning grave, pointed, and my eyes swung in that direction, and I blinked at the remains of Samuel Lonestar Bowman, wondering what I was supposed to be looking at.

"Evan, look out!"

I whirled around, Plum's cry ringing in my ears. Ndoro's foot lashed out, sent the shotgun spinning out of the way, and his huge hands gripped the garden shovel, swinging it like a battle-ax, swinging it at me.

Chapter 17

"**The rest of** it was nothing special," I said. "Just a matter of procedure, really."

"Procedure."

I nodded. "We had to leave the country, and I couldn't very well use my own passport, since I was officially dead. Plum went to see the MMM people, but it turned out that they were all in jail."

"Still?"

"Not still. Again. Elizabeth finally commuted those sentences to life imprisonment, and that gave the junta the chance they wanted to defy her. They had a mass hanging, and when the MMM crowd showed up to protest it, they all wound up in prison. So I had to bribe a freighter captain to get us to Johannesburg."

"Johannesburg?"

"Well, I have some friends in Johannesburg."

"And then from Johannesburg you came home."

"Well," I said, "not directly. First we had to go to Geneva. There's a clinic not far from there where they do extraordinary work. They've had wonderful success with personality disorders, and the doctor I spoke to said he thought they would be able to work wonders with Jane."

"Jane?"

"Sheena."

"You didn't leave her in Griggstown?"

"Well, how could I? I didn't think the Penners would be that happy to find her there, and besides she was basically a good person underneath, and she'd had a terrible life, and—"

"And after all you were married to her."

"Oh, for Christ's sake, Kitty—"

She made a *moue.* Girls are forever making *moues* in books, but I had never seen one made in real life before. There was a time when I thought they were French desserts. A chocolate moue, *s'il vous plait,* and a small cognac. Kitty made a *moue* as if she had had considerable practice doing just that. Then she took a short sip of wine and a long look at me.

"You went to Geneva," she prompted.

"I had to go to Zurich anyway. To turn the bearer bonds and negotiable paper into cash and put part of it in my account there."

"Part of it?"

"Well, part of it went to the clinic in Geneva. And part of it went, uh—"

"To Griggstown to finance the work of the MMM," she supplied. "Don't gape. How long have I known you? A long time, Evan. Where else did part of it go?"

"That's all."

She nodded encouragingly. "So then you came on home."

"Not exactly. I had to stop off in Amsterdam and sell the diamonds."

"And from Amsterdam—"

"Dublin," I said doggedly.

"Dublin?"

"I have trouble getting into England. You know that. From Dublin I took the ferry across the Irish Sea. Then we went from Liverpool back into Wales. Glamorganshire, to be specific. We went to this little town called Llundudllumellythludlum—"

"Oh, *that* little town. *We?*"

"Plum and I."

"I'd almost forgotten about her. You took her to Gǃublublub? Why?"

I explained. I took Plum to the little Welsh town because the more I thought about it the more I realized there was no other sensible place for her. She was obviously out of it in Modonoland, neither black nor white in a land where the twain never met, and where neither black nor white had it too good anyway. And while the Cape Coloreds in Capetown might have made a place for her, it was a place I wouldn't have wished on anyone. Nor did I think the good old U.S. of A. was quite what she needed to fulfill herself.

"But she has relatives all over Glamorganshire," I told Kitty. "On her father's side. The Welsh Nationalists I put her in touch with were all excited at the idea of digging up relatives of hers. She'll fit in perfectly. Since she's the only colored person for miles around she won't have to worry about prejudice. There's never prejudice anywhere unless there's a good-sized group to focus it on."

"So Plum is in Wales."

"That's right. In—"

"Please don't say the name of the town again."

"I was going to say the name of the county."

"Don't say that either. She's in Wales and Sheena's in Switzerland. You've managed to scatter your wife and your under-age mistress far and wide, haven't you?"

I tried to make a *moue*. It didn't work. I looked at Kitty, and she looked at me, and I shrugged.

"At any rate," I said, "here I am. I went back to Dublin and got a plane straight to New York. I'm back."

"So you are."

"And I'm ready to put both my feet on the ground now," I said. "I've had a chance to work everything out in my mind. About you and me and Minna and, oh, everything. We'll get married, Kitty. You and I. Married. And we'll adopt Minna and make a sensible home for the poor kid. And we'll move out of this godforsaken jungle of a city and get a nice little house in the suburbs. A home, a real home for the three of us. With a lawn and trees and a finished basement and aluminum storms and screens and—"

"What in hell is an aluminum storm?"

"You know, those combination windows. Storm windows. I don't know what they are. They advertise them in the Sunday *Times* in the section where they offer termite inspections. Whatever they are we'll have them. We'll have a sane life, that's what I'm getting at, a sane and healthy life for both of us, for the three of us, and we can have more children of our own, and maybe a dog, any kind of dog you want, you can pick out the dog—"

I sort of trailed off. She was looking at me with a very strange light in her eyes, and my voice seemed to be echoing oddly in my ears. "Any kind of a dog," I said, trying again, and let it trail off again because it was not going well.

She said, "You must be out of your mind, Evan."

She said, "A wife and children and a house in the suburbs. A washer-dryer and a refrigerator-freezer and an aluminum storm. Evan, if you honestly think that's what you want, then you'd better make an appointment with that brilliant doctor in Switzerland."

She said, "You decided you needed all that because you were stuck there in the middle of the goddamn jungle and everything was going wrong. 'I'll go back and settle down with Kitty,' you decided. 'No more running around like a nut. Instead I'll go settle down with good old Kitty.' That's very flattering, Evan. I feel like a social security benefit. Something to retire on."

She said, "For God's sake, after a week of pulling crabgrass you'd run screaming back to New York. What would you even *do* out there? How would you make a living? Oh, sure, I can see you putting on a shirt and tie every morning and riding the train to New York and doing something creative in an ad agency. Writing soap commercials or something. You'd absolutely love that."

"I—"

"And then you would take the train home, and read the paper and play with the kids and grill hamburgers in the yard, and then when we went to sleep you would sit around for eight hours counting your blessings, and then you could go back and write some deodorant commercials. Who are you kidding?"

"We wouldn't have to live in the suburbs. We wouldn't have to change our lives completely."

"We could get married and stay here."

"If that's what you want."

"And live the way we've always lived, except that we would be true to each other, and you would keep both feet on the ground, and we'd establish a sane living pattern and build a positive future together."

"That's exactly right, but the way you make it sound—"

"Evan, will you for Christ's sake wake up?"

I looked at her.

"You I should marry yet. With your cockamamie organizations and your twenty languages and staying up all day and night. With your two sons in Macedonia and your crazy wife in Switzerland and your daughter who isn't your daughter and your Welsh *schwartzeh* mistress young enough to *be* your daughter, and all your *mishegahs,* with all of this I should marry you? What kind of—"

"Why are you talking like that? You're not Jewish."

"What should I do in Armenian? Starve?"

"Kitty—"

"Oh, God, Evan, how could you be anybody's husband? How? You're all these different people all at once. You couldn't be a husband, Evan. I couldn't marry you."

She ran out of words, and I started to say something but nothing came out. We sat there for awhile and looked now and then at each other and now and then at the walls. I had some wine. She had some wine. I opened another bottle. She opened the window. I went to see if Minna was sleeping. Minna was sleeping. I came back and sat down and had another glass of wine.

I said, "I thought you wanted to get married."

"So did I."

"Are you going to marry him? That dishwasher?"

"He's an assistant cook."

"Whatever he is."

"I said no. He asked me again, and I said no, that I couldn't marry him. He wanted to know why. I almost told him. *You're a very boring person, you're sweet but you're boring.* That is what I almost told him, but I thought, oh, why be cruel to him? It wasn't his fault that he was boring. I told him I was sterile. You would have thought I told him I had syphilis or something. Do you remember Rima? You used to call her the Bird Girl?"

"I remember."

"They're seeing each other now. He'll propose and I know she'll say yes, she's really desperate. And I'm sure they'll have fifteen children all with their noses running and they'll be very happy together."

"I don't understand, Kitty."

She looked at me, shrugged. "Oh," she said, "I don't know. I couldn't marry him because he was too dull and I can't marry you because you're not dull enough. And I'm twenty-five years old, and that's one of those dumb ages that seems as though something major is due to happen to you. Sometimes it seems young and sometimes late at night it seems very old, and, well, my mind does weird things."

"Uh-huh."

"Twenty-five isn't so goddamned old, is it?"

"It's a hell of a lot older than fourteen."

"You crazy son of a bitch," she said, and I laughed, and she laughed, and I reached for her and she only hesitated for a minute.

A little later she said, "Hey, you nut. You would make the worst husband in the world."

"I guess you're right."

"I know I'm right. You'd get up in the middle of dinner and go halfway around the world to start a revolution. The worst husband in the world. But you know something else?"

"What?"

"You make a pretty groovy lover."

"And that's just as good?"

"Well, it's not as permanent. It isn't what my mother has been wishing would turn up for me for the past twenty-five years. But there are times," she said, burrowing close, "when it is very nice indeed."

That about covers it. The Chief turned up within a week, and as usual he wasn't wearing a plaid hat. I told him that Samuel Lonestar Bowman and Knanda Ndoro were both irretrievably dead. He was sorry to hear it, but said it was as he had anticipated.

"Never should have sent you in the first place," he

said. "Good money after bad. Damned foolishness. Wasting you on a mission like that one."

He asked about Sheena, said he'd had reports that the terrorist band had been dispersed. I let him draw the facts out of me—that Bowman and Knanda Ndoro had died at Sheena's hands, that I had been captured by the cannibals, and that I had put Sheena and her crew out of commission in the process of escaping. If I had just come out and said this it would have sounded like something Hercules did after he cleaned out those stables, but instead I let the Chief say it, and I sort of nodded in agreement from time to time.

"Capital," he said finally. "Those terrorists were a threat, you know. To the stability of the present regime. So you might say that you've helped keep the Modono-land government in business."

"Er," I said.

"And Lord knows," he said, refilling our glasses, "that they need all the help they can get. As a matter of fact they may be a lost cause. There's been a heavy run of arms into the country in the last week or so. The liberal opposition is looking stronger than ever. A new influx of funds, it seems. From Moscow or Peking, you would think, but our so-called experts admit they don't know the source."

I did, though.

Oh.

I almost forgot.

Back in the cemetery, with me standing there like a dead tree and Knanda Ndoro ready to chop me down. With the shovel whistling through the air at me.

I ducked. Just barely, and with no room to spare, but this was one of those instances in which a miss and a mile are of equal value. The Glorious Retriever missed, and I guess he hadn't expected to miss—humility, as he himself had attested, was not his long suit. Anyway, his momentum sent him stumbling, and perhaps the opium in his system had an effect and perhaps it didn't, but in any case he took a series of shuffling steps and wound up in the grave.

The shovel landed on top of him.

More precisely, the business end of the shovel conked him on the top of the head. I don't know if he was unconscious when he fell into the pit or no, but he was certainly out colder than a refrigerator-freezer after the shovel got him.

We couldn't wake him up. Plum didn't see why we ought to, and I could see her point, but oddly enough I couldn't work up much of a hate for the Retriever. He had saved our lives, whether or not he had intended to do so permanently. I couldn't completely shirk a feeling of obligation to him. And, on a more pragmatic level, his presence in Modonoland could only be awkward.

So what I wanted to do was get him out of the grave and onto his feet and away from there.

None of which I managed. He simply wouldn't wake up. I called his name and slapped his face and did everything I could think of. Nothing had any discernible effect whatsoever. He was out and he stayed out.

And it was getting light.

I tried lifting him, and that didn't work either. He was too big and too heavy and too limp to budge. So

I lifted the strongbox instead, which was easier, and Plum and I got out of the cemetery and carried the loot and the shotgun and the flashlight and the shovel back to the Penner house.

I bought smelling salts at a chemist's shop, and we went back to the cemetery around ten in the morning. But we couldn't get close to the grave, because somebody was already there.

The gravediggers. The three drunken gravediggers, passing a pint bottle back and forth, and laughing inanely, and staggering. And filling in that empty grave all the way to the top.

When they left, finally, arms linked and voices raised in song, I walked over to the grave. In the daylight I could read the little headstone. Gerhard Herdig, it said, and the year he was born and the year he died. I subtracted the one from the other and established that Herdig had lived to be eighty-two, which was more than the years of Bowman and the Retriever added together.

"May he rest in peace," Plum said. "Can we go now, Evan?"

I couldn't write on Gerhard Herdig's stone. But I knew what the Retriever would want, because he had come right out and told me. I stood at his graveside and bowed my head and spoke Robert Louis Stevenson's epitaph into the still morning air.

> *Under a wide and starry sky,*
> *Dig my grave and let me lie.*
> *Glad did I live and gladly die,*
> *And I laid me down with a will.*

This be the verse you grave for me:
Here he lies where he longed to be;
Home is the sailor, home from sea,
And the hunter home from the hill.

Plum said it was pretty Bugs Bunny. I told her she meant Mickey Mouse, and I told her I knew it was, and I told her to shut up.

Afterword

Evan Michael Tanner was conceived in the summer of 1956, in New York's Washington Square Park. But his gestation period ran to a decade.

That summer was my first stay in New York, and what a wonder it was. After a year at Antioch College, I was spending three months in the mailroom at Pines Publications, as part of the school's work–study program. I shared an apartment on Barrow Street with a couple of other students, and I spent all my time—except for the forty weekly hours my job claimed—hanging out in the Village. Every Sunday afternoon I went to Washington Square, where a couple of hundred people gathered to sing folk songs around the fountain. I spent evenings in coffeehouses, or at somebody's apartment.

What an astonishing variety of people I met! Back home in Buffalo, people had run the gamut from A to B. (The ones I knew, that is. Buffalo, I found out later, was a pretty rich human landscape, but I didn't have a clue at the time.)

But in the Village I met socialists and monarchists and Welsh nationalists and Catholic anarchists and, oh, no end of exotics. I met people who worked and people who found other ways of making a living, some of them legal. And I soaked all this up for three months and went back to school, and a year later I started selling stories and dropped out of college to take a job at a literary agency. Then I went back to school and then I dropped out again, and ever since I've been writing books, which is to say I've found a legal way of making a living without working.

Where's Tanner in all this?

Hovering, I suspect, somewhere on the edge of thought. And then in 1962, I was back in Buffalo with a wife and a daughter and another daughter on the way, and two facts, apparently unrelated, came to my attention, one right after the other.

Fact One: It is apparently possible for certain rare individuals to live without sleep.

Fact Two: Two hundred fifty years after the death of Queen Anne, the last reigning monarch of the House of Stuart, there was still (in the unlikely person of a German princeling) a Stuart pretender to the English throne.

I picked up the first fact in an article on sleep in *Time* Magazine, the second while browsing the Encyclopedia Britannica. They seemed to go together, and I found myself thinking of a character whose sleep center had been destroyed, and who consequently had an extra eight hours in the day to contend with. What would he do with the extra time? Well, he could learn languages. And what passion would drive him? Why, he'd be plotting and scheming to oust Betty Battenberg, the Hanoverian usurper, and restore the Stuarts to their rightful place on the throne of England.

I put the idea on the back burner, and then I must have unplugged the stove, because it was a couple more years before Tanner was ready to be born. By then a Stuart restoration was just one of his disparate passions. He was to be a champion of lost causes and irredentist movements, and I was to write eight books about him.

The first six Tanner novels, from *The Thief Who Couldn't Sleep* through *Tanner's Virgin* (nee *Here Comes a Hero*) were published as mass-market paperback originals by Fawcett Gold Medal. While they were being written and published, I was also publishing hardcover fiction with Macmillan, starting with *Deadly Honeymoon* in 1967. And, when I was ready to write a seventh book about Tanner, I offered it to Macmillan.

Nowadays, almost anyone would assume that the move from paperback original to hardcover was a Big Step Up. And nowadays it generally is. But things were different then, and the most significant reason for Macmillan's publication of *Deadly Honeymoon* was that Gold Medal had already turned it down.

Consider the numbers. Gold Medal paid an advance representing a royalty on the total number of copies *printed*, and generally amounting to somewhere between $2500 and $3000. (If they went back for a second printing, they paid a similar advance for all copies printed. This, sad to say, never happened with any of the Tanner books.)

Macmillan's advance was $1000, against royalties on copies sold, and in return they took 50% of any paperback earnings the book might generate.

Now there were compensations. Macmillan always took me out to lunch. And hardcover books were much more likely to get reviewed, for whatever that's worth. (Not much, I suspect.) And, finally, there was something far more prestigious about hardcover publication. A hardcover book with one's name on it—and perhaps one's photograph on the flap, or even the back cover—looked good on the shelf, and made one's mother proud. It was evidence that one had arrived, even though it might in fact owe its existence to one's having been first rejected by a paperback house.

Me Tanner, You Jane hadn't been rejected by Gold Medal. They seemed perfectly willing to go on publishing Tanner's adventures. The books weren't selling terribly well—as I said, none of the six ever managed to get into a second printing—nor did sales seem to be increasing from one book to the next.

For my own part, I was getting tired of the books—although I'm not sure I was aware of it at the time. For all that the settings changed from book to book, the characters and situations seemed to me to be repetitive. And, annoyingly enough, Tanner wasn't making me rich or famous, and for all that Fawcett was selling upwards of a hundred thousand copies of each title, I never had the sense that anyone out there was actually reading the books, or paying any attention to them.

So my agent and I put our heads together, and one of us—I forget which one—thought perhaps it was time to move Tanner to hard covers, and the other figured it was worth a try. By this time I had an idea and a title, and my agent arranged for me to meet with my editor at Macmillan and pitch it.

My first editor at Macmillan was a woman named Mary Heathcote. She bought and edited *Deadly Honeymoon* and *After the First Death,* and moved on before the latter book was published. Her replacement was Alan Rinzler—"I am the new Mary Heathcote," his note to me began—and it was to him that I would propose *Me Tanner, You Jane.*

We'd met before, of course, and had had lunch once or twice. He didn't drink, didn't drink at all, which I found quite remarkable. I thought everyone in publishing drank. I thought it was part of the job description.

Still, he was a bright and personable fellow, and his status as a nondrinker meant there was no great danger in meeting with him in the middle of the afternoon. (CBL read the notation on a good many cards in the Rolodex of one agent I knew; Call Before Lunch was what it stood for.)

So I went in and sat across the desk from him, and started talking about this book I planned to write, furnishing him while I was at it with some background on the series, and it didn't seem to be going too well. He looked, dare I say it, hungover.

And his eyes did look to be glazing over, which I've never found to be a good sign. So I talked a little faster, and fabricated some plot elements, and just kept talking, talking, talking, until the poor man held up a hand.

"Stop for a minute," he said. "See, I had some really dynamite hash last night, and I'm not tracking all that well today. But I can see you've got a well-thought-out story here, and it sounds good to me, so I'll put through a contract."

So then all I had to do was write the thing.

I don't remember a great deal about the writing of *Me Tanner, You Jane,* and I can't blame it on hash, neither dynamite nor corned beef. I picked the African setting in an effort to make the book different from others in the series, and looked for a dramatic way to get things going. In *The Scoreless Thai,* I'd kicked things off with Tanner locked in a bamboo cage suspended in the air, and awaiting execution; *Me Tanner, You Jane* begins with him already buried.

The opening sequence gave me a chance to use something that had been stuck in my head for a couple of years. While I was living in New Brunswick, New Jersey, I made the acquaintance of a Latvian painter named Valdi Mais. (I had recently published *Tanner's Twelve Swingers,* which involves the Latvian Army in Exile, and a local review of the book had led him to invite me to a party.) His English was good, if accented, but he made an interesting mistake on one word, adding the wrong suffix to a verb form; *comparison* came out *comparisment.*

I really loved that, and I wanted to have a character make errors of that sort, but I never was able to conjure up another example. So one of the chaps involved in Tanner's premature interment says comparisment for comparison. Good, I thought to myself. I've used it, and now I can forget about it.

But evidently I haven't.

*   *   *

Looking back all these years later, it strikes me that having Jane call herself Sheena after the comic book character may be more than happenstance. Because I've long felt that there's a comic-book aspect to this particular novel. (You could perhaps say as much for the whole series, but I think it's truest for MTYJ.) I have a feeling the same thing happened to me when I was writing the book as when I was pitching it to poor Alan Rinzler. I imagined the reader's eyes glazing over, and tried to bring him/her back by making every plot turn a little more outrageous.

I don't dislike the book all these years later, not by any means, but by the time I finished it I knew I was done—not just with the book itself, but with the series. I'm sure I'd have changed my mind if it had been a huge success, or even a rather small success, but all it did was come out and sell a handful of copies and vanish. It didn't even manage to get reprinted in paperback.

What it did do, oddly enough, was remain in print. Nowadays books get remaindered almost before the ink is dry; unless a book continues to sell at a pretty good pace, a publisher drops it from his list and ships the leftover copies to a cut-price wholesaler, and the next thing you know your novel is on the Bargain Books table at Barnes & Noble, pegged at about half the price it commands in paperback.

It was not ever thus. Until the government changed the rules, a publisher could keep a book in print as a service to readers and booksellers while still writing off the greater portion of costs for tax purposes. Some swine took the trouble to close this useful loophole, and that was the end of that.

But *Me Tanner, You Jane,* published in 1970, was still available from Macmillan seven or eight years later. I knew this because a copy actually sold, *mirabile dictu,* and I got a royalty check for forty-nine cents. If I'd had any sense—and a few hundred dollars worth of risk capital—I'd have stocked up. I had neither, and all I did was tell Otto Penzler, who promptly stocked up. Shortly thereafter the book disappeared.

And here it is, all these years later, in a handsome paperback edition not that much more expensive than the original Macmillan hardcover.

I do hope you enjoyed it.

Lawrence Block
Greenwich Village

Enter the World of Lawrence Block's Evan Tanner

Lawrence Block is widely acknowledged by both fans and reviewers to be one of the best mystery writers working today. He is also one of the most prolific, and his varied series—from the lighthearted romps of Bernie the Burglar, to the angst-ridden travails of Matthew Scudder the ex-cop, to the cool musings of Keller the Hit Man—have impressed readers with their versatility. He is a Mystery Writers of America Grand Master and a multiple winner of the Edgar® and Shamus awards.

But before the Burglar, Scudder, and the Hit Man, there was Evan Tanner—the most unusual spy who ever lived! Tanner hasn't slept a wink since a piece of shrapnel destroyed the sleep center in his brain, allowing him to get up to all sorts of trouble. BookPage calls the series "lighthearted . . . reminiscent of the tongue-in-cheek novels of Donald Hamilton (the Matt Helm series) or even Ian Fleming's classic James Bond stories," while the Rocky Mountain News *says, "Block is a true pro at coming up with offbeat adventures and peopling them with fascinating characters."*

Read on, and enter Tanner's world! . . .

The Thief Who Couldn't Sleep

A wake-up call is the last thing that Evan Tanner needs. Champion of lost causes and beautiful women, Tanner hasn't slept a wink since the sleep center of his brain was destroyed. And with the FBI keeping tabs on him, the CIA tapping his phone, and a super-secret intelligence agency wanting to recruit him, keeping wide awake is definitely a smart choice.

An alarming cause is the last thing Evan Tanner needs. But when he hears about a fortune in gold that's just waiting for him to liberate it, he's off. Getting across international borders, though, proves to be a difficult chore, especially when there's all that loot to carry as well. Not to mention the law, which is one step behind him and quickly catching up.

The Canceled Czech

Edgar® Award-winning author Lawrence Block delivers the second suspenseful romp featuring one of his most popular characters: Evan Tanner. With a shocking array of talents and no need to sleep, Tanner poses as the perfect secret agent—to treat a Nazi war criminal to an early withdrawal.

Janos Kotacek has been imprisoned by the Czech government and will no doubt be tried and hanged for his crimes. But to the super-secret intelligence agency that Tanner occasionally works for, Kotacek is worth more alive than dead. Tanner's orders are simple: go to Prague . . . storm a castle . . . free a criminal. That, of course, is the easy part. Keeping himself and his captive alive will take all of Tanner's waking hours. Good thing he's got some to spare.

Tanner's Twelve Swingers

——————

Globe-trotting spy Evan Tanner has just accepted a daunting assignment: He's agreed to find a heart-sick friend's long-lost love—and smuggle her out of Russia.

Everyone Evan meets on his trek across Eastern Europe is desperate for a one-way ticket to America—and for many of those people, he's the only hope. There's a subversive Yugoslavian author, a six-year-old future queen of Lithuania, and the beautiful woman Evan's been sent to rescue—a sexy Latvian gymnast who wants to bring her eleven swinging teammates along for the ride.

Now Evan has to find a way to get his unruly brood of political refugees safely onto U.S. soil. Some might say it's an impossible task, but Evan always finishes what he's started—even when his own life is on the line. . . .

The Scoreless Thai

_____

Would you believe Evan Tanner in the guise of a slightly batty butterfly collector?

Trotting through the woods, flailing his net?

You would? So did nearly everyone else.

Everybody except the band of guerilla bandits who decided it was safer and saner to snare Tanner than to let Tanner snare butterflies. They stripped him, stuffed him into a cage and told him: "Upon the rising of the sun, we will lead you to the chopping block and sever your head by driving the blade of an axe through your neck. . . ."

Tanner's Tiger

—————

Minna might be heiress to the Lithuanian throne, but she was still a little girl—one who was just thrilled about going to the World's Fair in Montreal. How could Evan Tanner know that this innocent outing would lead him and Minna into the middle of a terrorist plot? And not just any terrorist plot, but the most daring, most dastardly plot of all time . . . to blow up the Queen of England!

Tanner's Virgin

———

Evan Tanner loves lost causes and beautiful women. The FBI has a thick file on him, the CIA taps his phone, and a super-secret intelligence agency wants him to be their man! How can Evan Tanner turn down the urgent plea of a mother in distress—especially when the mother has a daughter as beautiful as Phaedra Harrow? Phaedra has disappeared into the hands of white slave traders somewhere in the Afghan wilderness. And Tanner, it appears, has no choice but to find her. . . .

Me Tanner, You Jane

Superspy Evan Tanner's newest assignment is to bring back alive the missing ruler of a new African nation . . . and the state treasury that's missing with him. But waiting in the heart of Africa is Sheena, a missionary's renegade daughter with an appetite for men and power, a taste that puts Tanner in the lovely arms of this deadly lady and lands him in hot water—the kind that can turn a spy into a cooked goose.

Tanner on Ice

Once, Evan Tanner was known as the thief who couldn't sleep, carrying out his dangerous duties for a super-secret intelligence agency. Then someone put him on ice—for about twenty-five years. Returning to the world (and trying to catch up with a quarter century's worth of current events), Tanner is about to embark on a new covert assignment that will take him to the exotic Far East, where mystery and menace are a way of life. . . .

Now, whether he's dodging double crosses or disguising himself as a monk, Tanner is learning that when it comes to power games, pretty women, and political wrangling, some things never change. And he's making up for lost time—with a vengeance.

Felonious fun with *New York Times* bestselling grand master

LAWRENCE
BLOCK